KING

AND OTHER CHILLING TALES

King and Other Chilling Tales

First Edition

This book is a work of fiction. Names, characters, places, and incidents either are products of the author's imagination or are used fictitiously. Any resemblance to actual events or locales or persons, living or dead, or living dead, is entirely coincidental.

Edited By: Shannon Gambino

Cover Photo By: Nate Merrit

Book Layout and Design: Jason Thacker

ISBN 10: 0692276688
ISBN 13: 978-0692276686

First Printing: August, 2014

Contents

KING

"Hurry up and go already, King!" begged Hal as he tried to convince his eight-year-old Golden Retriever to relieve himself on any of the several bushes in the backyard. Hal walked close behind as King sniffed for a place to leave his scent. He gave King's leash a gentle tug. "King, it's too cold for this." Hal didn't mind the coldness as much when King was just a puppy; the effects of middle-age seemed to have crept up on him over the last few years. Hal's brown hair had thinned out and turned grey, his body was much softer than it used to be, and his midline had grown outward.

At last, King chose a bush and hiked his leg high above his body. "All right. Good boy!" Hal pulled a cigarette from its pack and lit it. Even though Hal's wife, Maylene, had passed away eight years ago, he never smoked inside; she didn't like the way it made the house smell. Doing little things like this made Hal feel closer to Maylene. He'd never completely let her go and still felt her presence, sometimes.

After Maylene's death, Hal was introduced to six-week-old King by their daughter, Jen and her husband, Steve. They thought it would help take Hal's mind off the loss of Maylene and give him some companionship around the house.

Hal looked around the wooded hills in his backyard. Living deep in the Appalachian Mountains held many perks. Being an avid hunter and fisherman, he loved the outdoors.

The mountains seemed calm and peaceful until Hal heard a faint noise that came from the woods. He stood and listened. A subtle cracking sound made its way down the hillside. Hal and King stood still as they looked toward the noise. King started to growl.

"Shh. Be good, King. It might be a deer." King let out a disappointed whimper as he sat down next to Hal. The two of them stood together while the unknown creature continued popping twigs and rustling leaves as it crept closer to the edge of the tree line, about fifty feet away. Hal hoped to catch a glimpse of the noise-maker as he lifted his hand to shade his face from the orange glow of the street light at the side of the house. Just as his eyes focused, the sound stopped. Hal glanced around the edges of his yard in the hopes of seeing something; the darkness made it difficult to discern anything beyond the tree line.

After a few moments, nothing else happened. The hills once again became still, and the lonesome silence returned. Hal relaxed and looked at King. "Well, boy, I guess we'd better get back inside before we freeze to death out here." He took one long last puff on his cigarette and flicked it into the yard. King wagged his tail as he led his master toward the door.

The next night, just before bedtime, Hal and King

stepped out onto the back porch. Hal breathed in the crisp winter air and looked around. He noticed most of the snow that was in his yard earlier had nearly melted away. King looked back at his master, waiting for him to follow.

"C'mon, boy. Let's make this a quick one." The pair made their way to King's normal bushes at the corner of the house, next to the driveway. Hal pulled the cigarettes and lighter from his coat pocket and lit-up as King searched for a spot. Just as Hal put the cigarette pack and lighter back into his pocket, he heard the same crackling sound from the previous night. Hal stared into the darkness on the hillside. The sound traveled down through the woods to the edge of the tree line where it once again stopped. King sat next to Hal and sniffed the air. "What do you smell, boy?" Shielding his eyes from the street light again, Hal moved a couple of steps closer to the hillside. All of a sudden, a loud snort came from nearby. Hal stepped back from where he stood as King rose up and growled. "Take it easy, King." Hal continued to peer into the woods as he tried to figure out what made the noise. He had never heard any animal make that type of snorting sound before and wanted to find out what it was.

He and King stood there a few more minutes as they waited for the creature to make another move. Slightly unnerved and the freezing temperatures sinking into his bones, Hal turned toward the house. "Ah, let's get back inside. I guess it ain't gonna show itself again." King stood and continued to wait for something to come out of the woods. Hal gently tugged at King's leash and said, "Let's go." King obeyed and reluctantly followed him.

Later that night, Hal lay awake as he thought about

the snorting sound. He had encountered numerous animals in the wilderness during his lifetime, but nothing like that. Suddenly, King awoke from his sleep at the foot of the bed and growled. Hal opened his eyes and glanced at King, who was fixated on the window beside the bed. Hal sat up and patted the soft fur on his trusty dog's head.

"What is it, King?" he whispered. King continued to snarl at the window. Hal removed the thick patchwork quilts from his body and slid out of bed. King jumped down and followed. Hal crept to the window and slowly moved the blinds to peek outside. Frost covered the glass, making it impossible to see out. He tried to rub the frost away to clear his view.

"Hmph," Hal grunted as he discovered the frost was on the outside. He tiptoed through the house and tried to look out any of the windows, but frost covered each of them. Hal made his way back to his bedroom and sat on the edge of his bed as he listened for sounds. He worried that someone outside wanted to break in. Fifteen minutes passed without incident, and Hal decided it would be okay to lie back down.

Once settled back in his bed, he patted the mattress and called for King to come back to his spot. King leapt up and nestled down at the foot of the bed. The two quickly fell back to sleep.

Early the next morning Hal awoke to the buzzing of his alarm clock. Bleary-eyed, he rose from his warm, comfortable bed. As he stretched and scratched his back, King jumped down and made his way through the house. Hal bent over and turned off the buzzing alarm on his nightstand. He thoughtfully gazed at the picture of Maylene that sat next to the clock.

"Good morning, beautiful," he said with a smile.

Hal got dressed and made his way down the hall where he passed by all of the photos of Maylene, their daughter, and himself throughout the years. Hal loved glancing at each photo as he walked through every morning. It always made him face the day with a smile.

Hal entered the kitchen and looked into the living room at King curled up on the couch fast asleep, again. Hal chuckled, "Lazy dog".

Hal opened the refrigerator and took out some eggs, a loaf of bread, and a pack of bacon. He placed them on the counter and grabbed a couple of pans and two plates from the cabinet. He cooked in peace, and when finished, he heaped an equal amount of food onto each plate. He walked over and placed one plate on the table and called for King as he set the other plate on the floor. King jumped from the couch and ran over to his plate. Hal patted King's head as he said, "Here you go, boy. Eat up." and sat in the chair next to King. The two feasted on their breakfast together. As Hal ate, he thought back on the night before.

With his curiosity piqued, Hal hurried to finish his plate and said to King, "Let's go have a look around outside, buddy. What do you say?" King wagged his tail in approval. Hal reached his leathery hand over and stroked the golden fur on King's head as he smiled and said, "All right then, let's go." Hal leaned over, picked up King's empty plate and placed both dishes into the sink. He walked to the counter by the back door and picked up King's leash. King stood behind Hal, waiting. With King's leash in place, Hal grabbed his thick, black coat that hung by the door and put it on. He snatched up the lighter and the pack of cigarettes from the counter and put them in his pocket. Hal slipped on his already-tied shoes and opened the door. King walked out as Hal followed and closed the door.

Hal turned around and took in a deep breath of the cool, fresh mountain air. While Hal looked around, he thought back to King growling at his bedroom window the night before. He led King off of the porch toward the window. The sun didn't reach much of the backyard during the day, so some snow still remained there next to the house. Hal's attention turned to a couple of indentions, just inches from the house in the patch of snow at the base of the window. He and King arrived to the spot and inspected the strange outlines.

Hal lowered his brow as he cocked his head. The imprints seemed to be footprints of some sort and pointed toward his window. Hal shook his head; it looked so strange to him. The print looked like a large cat paw, but longer. Hal bent down and rubbed his fingers along the toe marks; just above them were four holes at the end of each toe. Hal assumed it to be from the creature's claws. He placed his pinky inside the first hole; nearly half of it filled the hole.

His eyes then moved toward the back of the print. It appeared the creature had a heel at the back of its foot, like a human. Hal knew there wasn't any cat, at least from his area with feet like that. A larger claw mark sat to the left of the heel. He rose up and scratched his head. King walked to Hal's side and sniffed the footprint. After a few sniffs, King turned to the side and hiked his leg toward the print. Hal chuckled and looked around the backyard at the other patches of snow. He noticed a few more prints in some of the other patches and began to trace a path that led up the hill to the tree line.

"Hmm." Hal suspected the prints must have come

from the creature that watched him and King over the past few nights. "Let's go, boy." Hal followed the prints to see where they went.

The two made their way up the hill and past the tree line. In the woods, more snow covered the ground, and the prints were easier to follow. The farther they traveled into the woods, the more Hal noticed the broken tree limbs beneath the prints in the snow. He stopped for a moment to examine some of the broken sticks. Most of them were small, but other sticks looked about two or three inches thick.

"King, whatever this thing is, it must be pretty heavy," Hal said as he held up one of the thicker sticks. "Let's keep going."

Hal and King continued to walk up the mountain for another thirty minutes until they came upon an old abandoned mine shaft. It was used a long time ago by some of the first coal companies that moved into the area many years ago. The tracks led straight into the dark cavern. King sniffed the tracks and pulled Hal toward the mine's entrance. Hal approached it and knelt down as he peered into the darkness. He sat there in silence while he watched and listened for any sign of life. A faint dripping sound came from inside the chasm, no doubt from the melting snow that seeped down from the ground above it. King stood brave at the entrance with his nose high in the air, still on the scent of the creature.

After a few uneventful minutes, Hal stood up and decided to make his way back to the house. "Let's get back home, King." King wagged his tail and turned to follow Hal. Along the way, Hal continued to glance over his shoulder and check the area around them. His heart pounded as thoughts of where the strange beast might be flooded his mind. He felt that at any second it might pounce on them. Unarmed, Hal regretted his decision to come in the hills without any protection for himself and his faithful pal. His steps were slight as he listened for noises and watched for any movement in the woods that surrounded them.

Hal stopped in his tracks. He thought he saw something move in the distance. King waited and looked up at Hal. Hal squinted and stared at the thick of woods in front of him. He wasn't sure, but he thought he saw movement out of the corner of his eye. He waited a moment; his heart pounded. A red fox scurried from behind a tree. Hal watched and let out a sigh of relief as the furry animal trotted through the woods. King whimpered as he too watched the fox move.

"That about scared me to death, King." Hal laughed at himself and continued on his way toward home. His pace increased a little after being scared by the fox.

Soon, he and King left the woods behind and stepped into the open space of their backyard. Relieved to see his home, Hal swore to never go in the mountains like that again without a gun. Hal did want to research the footprints a little more, so he decided to get the digital camera that his daughter bought him last Christmas and take a few pictures of the prints.

Once inside the house, King resumed his position back on the couch while Hal walked down the hallway and into his office to get his camera. It was put away in the second drawer of his desk. He picked up the silver device and turned it on to check the battery power. Once he assured himself the camera was ready to go, he went to the back door to put his shoes back on.

"I'll be right back, King." Hal opened the door and stepped outside. He walked over to the bedroom window and knelt down to get a good shot of one of the footprints. The camera flashed and made a beeping sound. Hal looked at its display to check his shot. He continued to take a few more pictures of some of the other prints in his yard. Content with what he captured, Hal went back into the house. Inside, King was lying by the door as he always did when Hal left the house.

"Let's go put these on the computer, buddy." King rose up and followed him into the office. Hal sat down and turned on the computer as King curled up next to him on the floor. Once the computer booted up, Hal inserted the SD card and began to upload the photos. Hal examined the prints a little closer. He zoomed in and out on each portion of the footprints several times.

"I think Roger should have a look at these."

He decided to print out a few of the images to show his closest friend, Roger Banks, a local game warden. While the photos printed, Hal walked into the living room and called Roger.

After a couple of rings, Roger's deep, raspy voice answered, "Hello."

"Hey, Roger, are you busy?"

"Nah. I just got in from work a little while ago. The old lady has just about finished making dinner."

"Oh, well I don't wanna bother you right now, but I got something here behind my house you might wanna have a look at."

"That so?"

"Yeah. It's some animal prints that I've never seen before. I snapped a few pictures for you to look at in case the snow melted before you got a chance to look at them in the yard."

"I might have to take a drive up there tomorrow and have a look then."

Hal nodded his head. "Sounds good, buddy. There's something else that kinda makes me wonder about them. The last few nights when I had King out to pee before bedtime, I've heard something come down to the tree line behind my house. Last night, whatever it was, made some awful sound, too. Nothing like I've heard before."

"Hmm..." Roger's voice altered from normal to a more serious tone. "That's weird."

Hal paced the floor as far as the phone cord allowed. "Yeah. I took King for a walk in the woods to follow these tracks a little while ago, and they led up to that old mine shaft way up near the top of the mountain."

"Hal, listen to me." Hal stood still. "Don't you be going back up in those hills until I'm there with you. Hear me?"

"Yeah, I hear ya. What's wrong?"

"I don't wanna sound crazy here, but there's been a couple of reports lately that's really got the wildlife team stirred up around here." Hal heard Roger's wife call him to dinner in the background. "Be there in just a minute, babe!"

"I'll let you go, Roger, and let you get some dinner."

"Hang on a minute, Hal. Walter Justice had a bunch of his livestock killed the other night. He said he came out when he heard his cows cuttin' a shine and saw some kind of weird animal tearing into one of them." Hal stood in the living room and gazed through his kitchen, out the sliding glass back door. "Some of the guys at work are trying to say the thing

Walter saw is called a Wampus Cat."

"Wampus Cat?"

"Yeah, it's an old Appalachian tale that goes back to the Cherokee Indians. It's a creature they called the Ewah. The story goes: A Cherokee woman didn't trust her husband much. So, one night when he was going out on a hunt with a group, she tried to disguise herself with the coat of a mountain lion. Well, she was caught by the men and punished. The tribe's medicine man transformed her into a monster, half-woman and half-cat."

"Sounds like a bunch of bull to me," Hal snipped.

Roger laughed and said, "Yeah well, that's just how the tale came about. It might just be a big cat or something. But either way, I saw Walter's cows, and there was something that tore them up that night." Roger paused for a second as his doorbell rang. "Crap. I guess the in-laws are here for dinner. I tell you what – I'll head up that way later and see if we can't get a glimpse at the thing tonight. That all right with you?"

"Sure is. Me and King won't mind having company over." Hal rubbed King's neck.

"All right, then. I'll be up there after dinner. As soon as I can get away, that is. See ya then, Hal."

"Okay, Roger. Bye-bye."

"Bye."

Hal hung up the phone and looked toward the back door.

"Wampus Cat, huh?"

He pushed his rocking chair in front of the glass door. He sat down and watched the hillside in hopes that the creature would make its way down during the daytime. King walked over and sat down next to Hal. Thoughts of the previous nights and the legend of the

Wampus Cat ran through his mind. Hal didn't believe the story, but he wondered if some strange, undiscovered creature did live in the mountains behind his own house. As Hal waited, he fell asleep in his chair.

Hal awoke to darkness. He yawned, rubbed his eyes, and looked at the clock on his stove; it showed 11:17 P.M. Still groggy, his eyes moved back to the door. An electric sensation ran through his body once his eyes focused on what stared back at him from his back porch. A black creature stood there: five feet tall and glaring at him with bright yellow eyes. Black fur thinly covered the top of the head and traveled behind to form a mane around its neck and chest. Its ears were pointed with small strands of coarse black hair that grew from the tips. The skin that covered the creature's long, humanoid face was stretched tight and was as black as the fur on its body. The ghastly creature snarled back its thin black lips revealing pointed teeth and fangs. In the middle of its face, a small bump for a nose protruded with slender holes for nostrils.

As the creature reached out its human-like arms and hands, it revealed long black claws that protruded from its fingertips. The monster let out a spine-tingling hiss that made Hal jump up and stand behind his chair. King barked ferociously at the creature. Hal tried to get King away from the door, but King refused to back down. The monster roared at King and began hitting the glass. Hal ran into the living room to call Roger. From there, he watched as the monster grabbed the doorknob and violently shook the door. After a few rings, Hal hung-up the phone and ran to his bedroom to get his shotgun. While in the bedroom, Hal heard the creature slam its body against the door; above King's barks, he heard the window cracking. With his gun in hand, he ran back into the kitchen where the monster continued its body slams into the glass. Hal aimed his gun and fired a shot through the door. Glass shattered and the creature fell off of the porch. Everything went silent again.

"Stay here, boy."

Hal eased toward the door looking for the creature. Shattered glass covered the floor inside the kitchen and outside on the porch. Hal peeked out in the yard, but didn't see anything. He stepped over the door frame, out onto the porch. He looked around, but still didn't see the monster. He made his way off of the porch and carefully looked around the yard. Suddenly, Hal heard the sound of crunching glass behind him, followed by King's threatening barks. Hal turned and ran inside the house to discover the creature had made its way to King and was trying to grab him. Hal didn't want to shoot again because King was too close. He ran at the creature and hit it with the butt of his shotgun. The creature growled and knocked Hal to the ground. As the creature turned, King lunged at it and sank his teeth into its arm. The hideous monster let out an agonizing cry. Angrier than ever, the creature jumped on top of King and picked him up under its arm; King whimpered as it bolted for the door.

Hal screamed for King as he struggled to get to his feet. Once Hal pushed himself off the floor, he ran out the door and frantically looked for the monster. He saw it carrying King up the hill toward the tree line. With no other choice, Hal raised his gun and aimed at the creature. He sighted in low and fired a shot. A burst of blood came from the creature's leg as it fell to the ground and dropped King. King seemed confused even though Hal called to him. King hesitated and looked over at the creature, then back at Hal; he limped cautiously toward Hal. Hal saw King's leg was bleeding from a pretty deep wound and ran over to meet him with his gun pointed at the monster. It began to rise up from the ground. Hal fired another shot into its back. The beast fell back to the ground, motionless.

"C'mon, boy, I need to get you some help."

He picked King up in his arms and packed him to his truck. Once there, Hal jerked the door open and laid King in the passenger seat and shut the door. Hal turned and ran to the driver's side. All of a sudden, he felt an excruciating pain in his back and collapsed onto the ground. The creature had gotten up, made its way to Hal, and dug its claws into Hal's back. He fought through the pain and managed to roll over to see where the beast may be. It had jumped off Hal and was trying to break the glass out of the passenger door's window.

"Get away from him!" screamed Hal as he struggled to his feet.

Hal realized he left the gun inside the truck when he put King inside. He searched the ground for a large rock. Hal spotted a baseball-sized stone at the edge of the driveway. He picked it up and charged the creature. Hal bashed the rock repeatedly into the monster's skull. The beast knocked Hal down and pounced on top of him. Hal wrestled with the beast and tried to strangle it. In the truck, King scratched and barked at the window. Hal continued to struggle with the creature for a few minutes; it gained the upper-hand, locked Hal's wrists to the ground, leaned over, and bit Hal's shoulder.

Abruptly, the monster rose from Hal and howled in agony. King managed to escape from the truck and attack it. King bit the creature as they fell beside Hal. Hal tried to get up, but he felt weak. The creature mauled King and once again picked him up under its arm. It ran toward the other side of the road. Hal lay on the ground screaming for King. As the creature raced to the end of Hal's driveway, Hal heard a familiar sound in the distance. He watched the creature run into the road where it was illuminated by two bright lights. The beast stopped to look; a brown SUV smashed into it. The beast and King flew through the air and landed several feet from the point of impact.

Tears flowed down Hal's face as he rose from the ground.

"King!"

Hal recognized the vehicle–it was Roger.

Roger slung the driver's side door open and yelled, "Hal! Was that the thing you told me about?"

"Yes! It had King!"

Roger and Hal ran over to King, who lay lifeless on the pavement. Hal bent over to pet King's head.

"I'm sorry, Hal. I didn't see them. I was in such a hurry up here."

Hal sat on the pavement with King as he ran his hand across King's silky fur. "Please no!" He cried uncontrollably.

Roger placed his hand on Hal's back. He looked up at the beast lying just feet from them, puzzled by its appearance.

Hal sobbed while looking down at King. King gradually opened his eyes and panted.

"King!" Hal smiled as his tears of sadness quickly changed into tears of joy. King slowly rose to his feet and licked Hal's face.

"Thank God, he's all right!" said Roger. As King and Hal celebrated having each other, Roger cautiously walked over to the creature. He used his foot to turn it over on its back. Startled by its appearance, he examined the beast.

"Hal, this is it: a Wampus Cat!"

"I don't care what it is, Roger. Just get it out of here. I don't want that thing near this house again."

"No problem, buddy. I'll have it out of here in just a second." Roger loaded it into a cage in the back of his SUV.

"Sorry I didn't get here sooner, Hal. I couldn't get away from my wife's family."

"It's okay. I'm just glad King's all right."

"Me too. I called for an ambulance; they're on their way, so let them take care of those wounds. All right, buddy?"

Hal laughed, "I will."

***

A month later Hal walked around outside with King as they always did just before bedtime.

"King, let's make this a quick one."

King sniffed as usual before he marked his territory when a loud cracking sound reverberated down the hill. Hal looked up into the dark woods and then down at King. He pulled a pistol from his pocket and walked over to the corner of the house.

"Let's see what's up there, King."

He flipped a large switch on the new electric box at the side of the house. All at once, the entire yard and hillside were illuminated by the six huge lights Hal had installed a few weeks earlier. He looked up toward the tree line and saw something standing there.

"Well look-a-there, King. It's a deer!"

As Hal watched the deer walk across the hillside, he felt a sense of peace that had been missing ever since Maylene passed away. He glanced at King, who stood faithfully next to him, watching the deer move.

"C'mon, boy, let's get back inside."

The duo made their way back into the house, turned out all of the lights, and laid down for a peaceful night's sleep.

THE REMEDY

Ian struggled to open his eyes as he felt the car come to a stop. His vision blurred as he glanced around; he recognized the Double Kwik convenience store sign.

"Hey now. I see you've got those pretty blue eyes open," Ian's newlywed wife Sarah said softly.

Ian sat up in his seat and rubbed his eyes. "How long have I been out?"

Sarah smiled at him from the driver's side and said, "Since we pulled out of the factory's parking lot."

Sarah had picked Ian up from work after his twelve-hour night shift was over. Ian glanced over to check the clock. It showed 8:07; he had been off work since 7:00.

After a long yawn, he asked, "Has traffic been that bad?"

Sarah laughed as she said, "No. I've stopped to pay a couple of bills on our way. You've been out like a light."

Ian watched an old man get out of a beat-up truck

and walk into the store. "I guess I have."

"I've gotta run in here real fast to get some milk, and then we'll be on our way home. You just lay your head back and get some more rest," said Sarah as she gently rubbed Ian's arm.

Ian smiled at her. "Want me to come in with you?"

Sarah checked her hair in the rearview mirror as she replied, "That's okay. You just lay back there and get yourself some more sleep." She took one last glance to make sure her makeup looked all right. She gently scooted over and kissed his lips. "I'll be right back," she said as she opened her door.

Ian leaned over the console as she got out of the car and whispered, "I love you, babe."

Sarah smiled and replied, "I love you, too."

Ian leaned back in his seat as she shut the door. He watched Sarah walk toward the store's entrance. The two of them had known each other since high school. They could finish each other's sentences and knew what the other thought by a simple change of expression. The two lost touch after high school when Ian moved away from their hometown of Pikeville, KY, to go to college two hundred miles away, and Sarah stayed home to attend community college. After a year, Ian dropped out and came back home to get a job in the local furniture factory. The two quickly rekindled their friendship and began dating shortly thereafter.

As Ian watched Sarah walk into the store, he felt the familiar feeling of completeness he got every time he looked at her. She stopped to hold the door open for an older woman. As Sarah stepped inside, Ian closed his eyes and laid his head back on the headrest. His thoughts wandered as he tried to fall back to sleep. Occasionally, he opened his eyes to look around. He no longer felt as tired as he did before his nap. Ian reached over to turn on the radio. He looked around at the people that entered and exited the store as he searched for a decent song. People seemed wrapped up in their own lives as they hurried to and from their vehicles. Ian was always an easygoing person and never understood why everyone seemed to rush through life.

Ian stopped on a station that was playing "Far Behind" by Candlebox. He sat back in his seat and fidgeted with Sarah's black hair bow that was twined around the gearshift. As he looked at the clock, he wondered just how long the lines were inside.

He thought to himself, "She only went in for a gallon of milk."

Just as he looked up, he noticed a man walk around from the back of the store. His slender physique moved fast. He looked to be in his early twenties. The man pulled up his baggy jeans covered with holes in the thighs and tugged down the white tank top he wore. He looked all around the parking lot as he approached the door. Ian watched as the man stopped just in front of the door and reached his hand behind his back. Ian sat straight up in the seat when he saw the man pull a large Bowie knife from the back of his pants. The thug grabbed the door and stormed inside. Ian froze as he realized the man was about to rob the store and might harm Sarah.

Without thinking of the possible consequences, Ian unbuckled his seat belt and pushed the car door open. He hurried as he slammed the door shut and rushed toward the store. His heart pounded, and thoughts of Sarah being hurt raced through his mind. He barely saw through the tinted glass windows in the front of the store. Just before Ian pulled the door open, his worst fear became reality. The man stood in front of the counter with one arm wrapped around Sarah's shoulders and the knife held to her neck by the other. His back faced the door.

Ian burst inside and stormed toward the man. The thug seemed to have been too busy demanding money from the cashier to hear the door open. Onlookers inside the store watched in horror as Ian approached the man. The robber noticed everyone looking behind him and turned with Sarah to see for himself. As soon as he turned, Ian slugged him right between the eyes. The robber stumbled back and released his grip on Sarah; Ian continued his onslaught on the man. Ian shoved him against the counter and delivered another devastating blow to his mouth. The man made a quick swipe with his knife. The knife slashed through Ian's forearm and made a deep gash. Ian's adrenaline numbed the pain, and the cut only made him angrier. The thug tried to stab Ian in his stomach, but Ian managed to grab his arm with both hands and twist it until he released the knife. Ian took the advantage and threw him to the ground; he dove on top of the man and pummeled him. Blood poured down Ian's arm from the cut as he punched the man's face. Soon, numerous gashes formed above and below the man's eyes.

Sarah stood back and watched as Ian pulverized the man. After they received the bulletin about the activated silent alarm, the police arrived on the scene. Two male officers pulled Ian off the robber. They quickly placed cuffs on the other man, pulled him to his feet, and walked him outside. The thug's face was covered with his own blood and the blood from Ian's knife wound. The man stumbled about as the officers led him to one of the ambulances that arrived. An older male officer walked with Ian to the second ambulance.

He held the door open for Ian as he said, "That was a brave thing you did back there, son."

Ian wore a nervous smile on his face as he replied, "Thanks. I was just protecting my wife."

He tightly held the bottom of his bloodstained, blue uniform shirt over the knife wound. The officer spoke to the female paramedic that waited by the back of the ambulance.

"He's got a pretty bad knife wound. I'm no expert, but I'm guessing he's gonna need stitches."

The paramedic waved Ian to come closer. She took Ian's hand off the cut and moved his shirt to examine the bloody gash.

Upon first sight the paramedic replied, "Yep. I'd say you're right about that."

Disappointed, Ian shook his head as he muttered, "Great."

Sarah emerged from the store still visibly shaken by the ordeal. She looked around for a moment until she spotted Ian. She walked over and asked, "Are you ok?"

"I'm gonna have to get stitches," said Ian as the paramedic continued to disinfect his cut.

Sarah stood reserved with her left arm across her stomach as she covered her mouth with her right hand and observed the cut on Ian's forearm.

"Oh my gosh, baby. I know that has to hurt."

Ian shrugged his shoulder and said, "Kinda. It's starting to sting more and more."

As the paramedic finished making a temporary bandage, she looked at Sarah and said, "Ma'am, you're welcome to ride to the hospital with him, if you want."

Sarah looked to Ian for the answer.

"You think you'll be all right to drive?" he asked.

She bit her bottom lip and nodded.

"Would you care to just follow us? That way after the doctor is done, we can just go home." asked Ian.

Sarah smiled as she said, "Yeah, that's no problem."

She leaned over and hugged him; Ian slid his good arm protectively around her waist.

Sarah followed the paramedics to the hospital, where they rushed Ian to a room inside the E.R. A couple of nurses walked in and out of the sliding glass door of Ian's room as they gathered information and vitals for the doctor. Sarah soon joined Ian inside just before the doctor and a nurse entered. The doctor held a doughnut in one hand as he looked over Ian's charts in the other. The nurse hastily prepared everything necessary for Ian's stitches.

"Good morning, Ian. How are you doing?" asked the doctor with a very thick Indian accent. He took a bite of his chocolate and sprinkle covered doughnut.

Trying to keep a positive attitude, Ian replied, "I'm tired. Just got off of work a little while ago."

The doctor placed his clipboard on the counter next to the washing sink and threw the rest of his doughnut into the garbage can.

"Well, my name is Dr. Hassip; this shouldn't take too long. We'll have you out of here in no time." He wiped his mouth and dark mustache with a paper towel and washed his hands.

The nurse rolled a small tray covered with various needles, bandages, and other supplies next to Ian, who sat on the examining table.

"That was a very brave thing you did at the store, Ian." She looked to Sarah and said, "You are a lucky woman to have such a heroic man for your husband."

Sarah smiled, "I know. He saved my life today."

Ian, very modest, thought of his act as just a duty to protect Sarah, as her husband.

Dr. Hassip snapped his gloves on and rolled a chair next to Ian. He started the excruciating procedure. Ian fought through the pain as the needle pierced though his skin with each stitch. He felt the thread drag through and pull the gaping wound together. Just as the doctor promised, the procedure progressed rapidly, and before Ian knew it, he was stitched. Dr. Hassip and the nurse left the room for a moment to finish Ian's paperwork and get him ready to check out.

Ian and Sarah sat in the room and talked about how quickly the doctor worked. Soon, a light rapping sound came from the glass door. Ian and Sarah looked and saw a slender woman with long, straight brown hair standing outside of the room, smiling at them. She wore a black business jacket, white shirt, and khaki dress pants. Confused, Ian and Sarah looked at each other as if they recognized her, but unsure from where. Sarah got up.

As she slid the door open, the woman asked, "Ian and Sarah Rogers?"

Sarah still wondered where she seen the woman before as she responded, "Yes?"

The woman held her hand out to shake Sarah's. "It's good to meet you. I'm Lynn Justice from WYMT News Channel 6. I'd like to get a few words from you both about Ian's heroics this morning."

Sarah then realized why Lynn looked so familiar and was very glad to meet her. "Sure, come in."

Lynn walked over and exchanged pleasantries with Ian. She told him how much she admired courageous people like him and wished there were more people that would stand up for what's right. Ian was very excited to meet Lynn, but remained very humble about what he did for Sarah. As Lynn started to ask him specifics about the ordeal, an urgent message came across the intercom.

"Attention doctors, we have a code blue in the E.R. I repeat. Code blue. Any available doctor please report to E.R. room six; that is emergency room six."

Lynn glanced around as a look of worry crept across her face. "I think that's–yeah, it's the other guy's room."

Ian looked at Lynn and asked, "What other guy?"

Lynn seemed to be very surprised they didn't know. "Steve Goins, the other man from the Double Kwik."

"You mean they brought him here? And he's just a few rooms down from us?" asked Ian, visibly upset by the fact.

"Yeah, I passed by his room on my way in," Lynn softly said.

Sarah panicked. "Oh my gosh! What if he knows we're right over here, and he tries to come in here after us?"

A couple of nurses ran by the closed glass door, followed by Dr. Hassip.

Lynn tried to comfort Sarah, "He won't be doing that. He looked like he was in pretty bad shape from what I could see."

Ian, still upset with the man, said, "Good. Maybe the scumbag will think twice next time he tries to hurt innocent people."

A few moments passed when another pleading message came through the intercom, "Attention! Security is needed in the E.R. Security is needed in the E.R.! Room six!"

Ian, Sarah, and Lynn all looked at each other.

"That's the same room!" said Sarah.

Lynn started toward the door. "I'm gonna go see what's going on. I'll be right back."

Lynn slid the door open as four security guards rushed down the hall. As she exited, Ian jumped off the examining table to shut and lock the door. They heard screams and a loud commotion down the hall. Ian thought the man was trying to make his way to them. He prepared himself if the thug tried to attack them again. He walked over to Sarah and wrapped his arms around her.

The two of them waited in the room. The sounds of distress started to fade away after a few minutes. Soon, Lynn returned to the door. Ian rushed to unlock it and to hear news of what happened in room six. Lynn seemed visibly shaken by something; no longer the same calm, collective woman she was before she left the room.

Concerned, Ian asked, "You all right?"

Lynn walked into the room and took a deep breath while Ian closed the door.

"Guys that man just lost it in there!" said Lynn.

"What happened?" asked Ian.

"At first, the nurse said she paged for a doctor because Goins lost all of his vitals. The man had no pulse and wasn't breathing at all. The doctor and nurse were checking him and giving him CPR. That's when he just started attacking them!"

"Do you think after they revived him, he was just in shock or something?" Sarah asked nervously.

Lynn shook her head as she replied, "That's just it. The nurse said his vitals never showed back up on the monitor. That poor doctor; while he was giving him mouth-to-mouth, the man bit off the doctor's entire upper lip."

"You have got to be kidding me!" said Ian. Sarah covered her mouth.

Lynn's eyes widened as she continued, "That's not the worst of it! Once I got there, he had already bitten into one security guard's neck and another's arm. The other two managed to restrain him on a gurney, but he was still trying to get to them."

"Wow, that's just crazy," added Ian.

Sarah moved her hand away from her mouth and asked, "What did they do with him?"

"They took him down the hall through the double doors. I'm not really sure where they went with him after that," said Lynn.

Sarah looked a little relieved to hear that. "Good. Let's get out of here while they've got him secured."

Ian agreed; he, Sarah, and Lynn walked out of the door and toward the emergency room exit. A security guard stopped them.

"I'm sorry guys, but the floor is locked down for a little while until the situation is under control."

Ian glanced to Sarah and Lynn.

The guard asked, "Please return to the room you were in. There will be someone to let you know when the lockdown is lifted."

The three of them returned to the room and waited.

"How long do you think they'll keep us here?" asked Ian.

"I don't know. I've never known this place to have a lockdown like this. Ever." replied Lynn.

A doctor wearing a white lab coat and a surgical mask knocked on the glass door. Lynn stood next to the door, so she unlocked it. The doctor stepped in, holding two syringes.

"Hello guys, I'm Dr. Holbrook. I'm going to need to get a couple of blood samples from Ian and Sarah." The doctor walked toward Ian.

Ian cringed at the sight of the needle. "What's going on Dr. Holbrook? Are we in any kind of danger?"

Dr. Holbrook lowered his brow and tried to assure Ian everything was under control. "We just need to take some blood samples from the people who have recently come into contact with Mr. Goins. After his incident, we received word from the lab that something suspicious showed up in his blood samples. We just want to take extra precautions to make sure he didn't pass this on to any other person." Dr. Holbrook stuck the needle into Ian's vein and drew his blood into the syringe.

Lynn stood back and watched. Something didn't seem to sit right with her about Dr. Holbrook's comment.

"What showed up, Doctor?" she asked.

Dr. Holbrook removed the needle from Ian's arm and held a cotton ball on the puncture site.

As he placed a bandage over the small wound and readied the second needle for Sarah, he explained, "To be honest, we're not sure. It looks like a genetic mutation of some sort; there is something in Mr. Goins' blood that is attacking all of the white blood cells, and at the same time, transforming the red blood cells into something we have never seen. We don't know if this is some kind of a virus causing it to happen or something that has lain dormant in his body until now."

Ian tightly closed his eyes as he shook his head. "So are you saying this virus, or whatever it is, caused him to go crazy?"

Dr. Holbrook nodded as he drew blood from Sarah. "It is very possible."

Ian's heart pounded. He thought to himself, "What if that guy infected me?" Dr. Holbrook finished drawing Sarah's blood and put a bandage on her arm. "Doctor, please let us know if you find anything," said Ian.

Dr. Holbrook hurried toward the door. "I'll let you know something the minute I find out." He walked out of the room.

Sarah rubbed her arm and asked, "Why was he wearing a mask?"

Ian and Lynn looked at each other, neither of them knew.

They tried to speculate and analyze everything that had happened as they impatiently awaited Dr. Holbrook's return. Nothing made sense, and every explanation they came up with only led to more questions. The emergency room was filled with an eerie silence that sent chills down everyone's spines.

The clock slowly ticked the minutes away; Ian grew frustrated.

"What is taking them so long? We deserve to know answers," said Ian as he paced the floor of the room.

All of a sudden, a group of people dressed in white hazmat suits unlocked the door and burst into the room. They came straight for Ian and grabbed him.

"Hey! What's going on?" screamed Ian as he tried to stop them from dragging him out of the room.

Sarah ran to Ian and yelled, "Where are you taking him?"

The people didn't say anything as they struggled with Ian and dragged him out of the room. Horrified, Sarah and Lynn ran out into the hall and followed the white-suited people as they forced Ian past the double-doors leading to a long hallway. The doors slammed shut just as Sarah reached them. She tried to open them, but they were locked.

Ian looked back and saw his wife and Lynn watching through the small window in the door as the group led him around the corner. The hallway continued for a long stretch and led to a door with a sign that read, "Authorized Personnel Only: Violators Are Subject To Legal Action." The group stopped as one of them swiped an identification card. The door unlocked, and the group continued into the room. It was very large and brightly lit. A few examining tables sat in the room, and several gurneys were placed randomly about.

As soon as the door opened, Ian heard painful screams coming from somewhere in the room. The screams didn't come from just a single person; Ian made out four distinctly different cries. He glanced around as the group seemed to be leading him to an examining table with restraints for the limbs and head. Ian at last spotted the source of the screaming. Dr. Hassip was strapped to a table, howling in pain; next to him were three unfamiliar people. The group lifted Ian onto the empty padded table and strapped him down.

"What is going on?" yelled Ian.

He couldn't see much around him with his head held down by the restraint. He heard a muffled, yet familiar voice coming toward him–it was Dr. Holbrook.

"I'm sorry if they scared you, Ian. I needed you to be separated from everyone else as quickly as possible."

Out of the corner of his eye, Ian saw another

person wearing a hazmat suit walking toward him; it was the doctor.

"Doctor Holbrook, please tell me what's going on!"

Dr. Holbrook stood next to Ian as he said, "Again, my apologies, Ian, but I'm afraid you've been infected by this unknown virus. It seems to be spreading rather quickly."

Ian's heart sank; he closed his eyes as tears filled them. "What's going to happen to me?"

"That's still up in the air right now. We're not sure when to expect this strange mutation to occur inside you. All we know is it will for sure happen; it's just a matter of time. That's why it's necessary to keep you restrained." Dr. Holbrook walked around Ian to check all of his restraints. "There's one thing that's puzzling me though"

Ian watched as Dr. Holbrook examined the restraint on his head. "What's that?"

"Well," Dr. Holbrook walked away as he continued to talk. "I don't understand what's happening with you. The mutation is there, but it seems to be taking much longer to affect any of your blood cells. Doctor Hassip, the nurse Melissa, and two security guards, Steve and Jose, have already lost all vital signs and are still living. I use that term very loosely. But with each infected person, the time frame of change seems to be around an hour or two." Ian could hear the keys of a keyboard clacking. "You came in contact with Mr. Goins well over that period of time–hours even!"

Ian tried to piece together everything Dr. Holbrook told him. He felt fine and not even the slightest bit sick.

"So do you think that means I might be immune to

it?"

Ian heard Dr. Holbrook fidgeting with something over to his left.

"I don't know, maybe. It's too soon to know that for certain." Dr. Holbrook approached Ian holding a needle. "I'm about to give you a sedation drug. It will work quickly, so you'll be out in no time. I need to do some more tests on you, and honestly, it'll hurt much less if you're asleep through them."

Before Ian said anything, Dr. Holbrook jabbed the needle into Ian's shoulder. Almost instantly, Ian felt himself slip off to sleep.

***

"Ian, wake up," said a female voice.

Ian felt a light tapping on his face.

"Come on Ian, we've gotta hurry," said a different female voice.

Ian blinked his eyes; his vision blurred.

As Ian's eyes began to focus, he was startled to see two people standing over him.

"He's awake! Come on, baby, we've gotta get you out of here."

Ian immediately recognized the voice–it belonged to Sarah.

Ian struggled to make his eyes focus as the other voice said, "All right. He's going to be a little groggy at first. Just give him a minute to adjust."

The other voice belonged to Lynn. Ian tried to move his arms once he realized the restraints had been removed.

"What are you guys doing?" mumbled Ian as he struggled to sit up.

"We're here to get you out of this place," said

Sarah as she held Ian's hand.

"What happened to Doctor Holbrook?" asked Ian.

"Everybody is gone, Ian, the hospital was taken over by those lunatics. We're lucky we were still able to get to you," said Lynn.

She and Sarah helped Ian to his feet.

Ian rubbed his eyes and asked, "What do you mean everybody's gone? What happened?"

Lynn seemed nervous, she looked around the room as she asked, "You ever seen that movie, *Dawn of The Dead*?"

Ian nodded.

"Well I hope you paid close attention to it, 'cause it's real now."

Ian's mouth dropped open as he looked at the two of them and said, "Really? You mean that guy turned into a zombie earlier?" Ian paused as he looked at both of them. "You're joking, right?"

Lynn shook her head, "I wish I were. It's gotten really bad since you've been out."

Ian looked on the walls of the room for a clock. "How long have I been out?"

"About four hours," said Sarah as she held Ian's arm to help keep his balance. "It's getting close to nightfall now. We've got to move."

Once Ian was ready, they made their way out of the room and into the hallway. The hospital was a wreck, with beds and wheelchairs littering the hallways and broken items everywhere. As the trio ran to the stairway, a small group of people dressed in the same white hazmat suits as before came charging up the hall; they were armed, packing automatic weapons. Sarah and Lynn ducked into a vacant room with Ian.

As the gun-toting people ran by the room, Ian

asked Lynn, "Do we have any guns?"

Lynn shook her head.

"Didn't you learn anything from the movie?" asked Ian.

The three of them continued to head for the stairway at the end of the hall. Once there, Ian pushed the door open. They ran through the door and started downstairs. They were frightened when they came across someone slumped over against the wall at the bottom of one flight. Ian saw the man sitting in a pool of his own blood.

Ian spoke to the man, "Hey, buddy, are you awake?"

The man slowly moved his head to reveal his face, coughed, and said, "Ian."

"Doctor Holbrook!" yelled Ian as he ran to the doctor's side. "We're gonna get you out of here." Ian bent over to help Dr. Holbrook.

"No!" yelled Dr. Holbrook. "I've been bitten." Ian stopped and listened to him. "It's no use, I'll be one of those things soon enough."

Ian looked at the bite mark on the doctor's hand. "What's causing this?"

Dr. Holbrook sat with his head against the wall. "It's a virus. It's transferred through the bloodstream. I never could pinpoint the exact reason our cells mutated it." Dr. Holbrook coughed hard. "If there was some way to find that out, then there is a good possibility a cure can be found. That's why the tests I did on you were so important, Ian."

Lynn and Sarah looked at Ian as he said, "What did you find?"

Dr. Holbrook struggled to catch his breath. "I was right; you do have the mutation in your blood, Ian. However, for some reason, you are completely immune to it. Your white blood cells are much stronger than any I have ever seen. After a few tests and some detective work, I found the key to all of this." Ian leaned closer to Dr. Holbrook; his voice faded into a whisper. "You are the main carrier, Ian. This has probably been in your body for your entire life, and that's why you are not affected by it. It wasn't until after Mr. Goins cut your arm and the blood from your cut mixed with several wounds on his face. Your blood was transferred to his, ultimately causing his mutation."

Ian looked at Dr. Holbrook horrified. He then looked to his wife and Lynn. They seemed to be as equally shocked by Dr. Holbrook's findings.

"So are you saying this is all my fault?"

Dr. Holbrook coughed twice as he said, "Well, to put it bluntly, it is. But, you can also stop this."

Lynn spoke up and skeptically asked, "How can anybody stop this, doctor?"

"Before the first of them got loose in the laboratory I was in contact with Dr. Dean Parker at Highlands Regional Hospital in Prestonsburg. He created a formula from the small sample of your blood I sent him. In every test, his formula was completely destroying the virus and reversing its effects. He just needs more of your blood to make enough to stop this outbreak. Please, get there. It's the only hope we have."

Dr. Holbrook looked to be fading fast; Ian and the others knew they needed to get to Dr. Parker quickly.

"What about you, Doctor?" asked Sarah.

"Don't worry about me, I did my part. I have no regrets. Just go, I want to stay here."

A horrendous wail came from above them; they heard something making its way down the stairs toward them.

"That's one of them! Get out of here before it's too late!" yelled Dr. Holbrook with what little strength was left.

Hesitant at first, the three listened to Dr. Holbrook. They granted his one last request and left him there to die in his own peace. The zombie staggered down the stairs; Ian, Sarah, and Lynn quickly descended the stairs to escape. A few moments later, they heard painful screams come from Dr. Holbrook as the zombie reached him.

Ian reached the first floor entrance. He grabbed the handle and tried to push it open–it was stuck.

"Great!"

Lynn instinctively thought of an alternate route. "Come on, we can reach the parking lot a lot faster through the basement, anyway."

Ian and Sarah were relieved Lynn knew that. They weren't familiar with the hospital's layout because they only came there for rare checkups and traveled the normal footpaths. They continued to run down the stairs. They had made it a few steps when Ian heard something below them.

"Hold up a second!"

Sarah and Lynn stopped and looked at Ian. He listened to a pair of slow footsteps coming up to them. Ian pointed down the stairs for them to listen.

"Is that one of them?" whispered Sarah.

"I don't know. It might be. We need to turn around," replied Ian.

He started to turn around and run when Lynn said, "Wait! That one is still up there with Doctor Holbrook. We're gonna have to get through to the first floor."

Ian and Sarah nodded as they began the short trip

back to the first floor.

Once they made it back to the door, Ian held the knob as he tried to shove it open. It budged, but something heavy sat in front of the door on the other side. They heard the footsteps creeping up toward them. Ian asked Sarah and Lynn to help him try to move whatever was in front of the door. Once all three of them pushed, the door started to move little by little.

Unexpectedly, all of the lights went out and caused a moment of total darkness in the stairwell. The three of them froze; the footsteps below were even louder without the humming from the florescent lights. Whoever was walking up the stairs didn't seem to care about the sudden loss of power. Seconds later, the emergency lights kicked on. The small lights above each doorway dimly lit the stairwell.

"We gotta get out of here!" said Lynn as she shoved her body against the door even harder.

Ian looked down to the next flight of stairs and almost jumped out of his skin. An older woman stood looking at him. He saw her shirt soaked with blood in the pale yellow light. Ian hesitated whether to ask her if she needed help; against his better judgment, he did.

The old woman opened her mouth as if she was about to say something, when a wicked hiss roared out. Ian nearly fell onto his back as he stumbled away from the rails. The woman instantly started after Ian. He turned and slammed his entire body against the door. Finally, the door opened enough for them to squeeze through. Ian let Sarah and Lynn go as he watched the woman make her way up the last set of stairs to them.

Sarah screamed when she got to the other side.

Once Lynn was through, Ian squeezed his body through the small gap. As soon as he stepped through, he saw what scared Sarah; a large man was wedged against the door. Several bloody wounds covered his upper torso. Ian leaned over the man's body as he barely slammed the door shut in time. They stepped back as they watched the old woman press her bloody face against the window, rake her teeth against the glass, and slap the door with her boney hands.

Ian stood in utter disbelief as he said, "This is my fault."

Sarah placed her hand on Ian's shoulder. "Ian, don't be like that. There's no way you could've known. Doctors didn't catch this in your blood, so how would you?”

Just then, Lynn spoke up, "Guys, we really need to get out of here. My van is parked right out front. It would be the quickest way out."

Ian took in a deep breath and agreed. Lynn turned and began to run; Ian and Sarah absently followed her.

The main entrance was right around the corner and down a small hall which led to the lobby. Some evening light trickled around the corner of the hall and dimly lit the area. The doors to the entrance were shut. As they approached them, Ian noticed an elderly man lying on the floor with a thick wooden cane propped up next to him. Ian thought it would make, at the least, a temporary weapon. He cautiously ran over to the man, as he tried not to disturb him, weary the man had already turned. Lynn and Sarah failed to notice Ian making his way toward the man as they continued to run toward the doors. Ian slowed down to a slight jog as he came closer to the man's body; he knew any wrong move would have the man up and ready to take a bite out of him. Sarah noticed Ian was no longer behind her about the time Ian leaned down to grab the sturdy cane.

"Ian! What are you doing?" she whispered.

Ian held his finger up, telling her to hold on. He knelt down and glanced at the man. His eyes were closed, and he wasn't breathing. Blood oozed from the old man's shoulder and glimmered in the pale light that shone through the large glass windows. The wound appeared fresh, so Ian knew the man hadn't been dead for very long. Ever so cautiously, Ian grasped the smooth wooden cane in his hand. Sarah and Lynn watched as Ian slowly rose with it. He took a few careful steps away, turned, and dashed toward them.

"Let's move," said Ian as he smiled and patted the cane against his hand.

The three made the short dash to the front entrance. With the electricity out, the sliding doors weren't operating. Ian placed his hands between the doors and pried them apart. He held them as Lynn and Sarah slid through. Ian soon realized things outside were far worse than expected. As soon as he opened the door, the piercing sounds of people screaming and blaring car alarms filled his ears. He moved out from between the doors nearly in a daze.

"My van is right over here!" yelled Lynn as she ran through the parking lot.

Ian took Sarah by the hand as they followed close behind Lynn. He saw the Channel 6 news van in the front row. They heard a feral growl come from the left side of the parking lot. Ian saw a bloody scalp as it bounced above the roofs of some smaller trucks.

"It's coming after us! Follow Lynn to the van, Sarah. Go!" said Ian just as the male zombie came into plain sight.

Sarah continued to follow Lynn, who'd already unlocked the driver's side door.

Ian saw enough zombie flicks to know the only way to kill these crazed monsters was to destroy their brain somehow. The zombie shambled around the last car and came after Ian. He stood and readied the cane like a major league batter about to unload on a speeding fastball. As the zombie neared him, he took a couple of steps forward to gain some momentum. Ian took a mighty swing just when the zombie came within striking distance of him. A loud crack came from its skull as the solid cane made impact. The zombie fell to the ground at Ian's feet. He stood over top of it as he delivered a few more blows to its head. Ian roared as he took out his frustrations on the zombie's face. The cane at last snapped into two pieces. Ian stopped for a second; he breathed heavily and looked at the broken piece he clenched in his hands. He heard the van start and back up. He glanced up for a moment and saw Lynn driving to him. Ian looked back at the zombie lying on the ground. Its arm twitched. He held the broken cane high above his head and jammed the broken, pointed edge into the zombie's skull. Ian rose up as he looked at the man, who lay lifeless. Blood oozed out around the cane sticking out of the man's forehead. The van came to a stop behind Ian.

"Are you okay?" asked Sarah. Ian nodded as he stumbled back to the van. He was shaken up by everything that happened.

Ian climbed inside the front of the van as Sarah scooted over to the middle of the cloth bench seat.

"I've got a feeling traffic is going to be horrible," said Lynn as she drove to the end of the parking lot and up to the red lights on the street.

Vehicles jammed the roadway as people tried to get out of Pikeville. Lynn decided to take an alternate route through town that took them a little further from the interstate, but led back around to a much less crowded section of it.

The ride through town seemed to take forever as they passed the devastation that surrounded them. Lynn drove around many abandoned and wrecked cars that sat in the middle of the road. People dashed up and down the sidewalks as they tried desperately to seek shelter from the flesh-hungry beasts that roamed the city. They neared the end of a two-lane bypass road that led to the interstate. Lynn slowed the van down as she saw three cars sitting in the middle of the road.

"What's going on here?" said Ian as he looked at the cars.

There appeared to be no way around them. The van's brakes squeaked as it slowly came to a stop about twenty feet from the parked cars. The cars seemed to be parked that way on purpose. The trio sat for a moment as they looked for someone to ask the reason for the road block. Ian decided to step out of the van to see if anyone was around.

"Hello?" he yelled.

"Ian, please be careful," Sarah whispered from inside the van.

Ian yelled again.

No one answered.

He walked in front of the van and approached the cars. With no way to get around the cars, it seemed like their only option was to turn around and fight the gridlocked traffic in town.

"That's great," said Ian as he turned to walk back

to the van. "Looks like we'll have to fight through the traffic in town."

Ian saw the disappointment on Sarah and Lynn's face as he approached the van. Without warning, two men stormed from behind the van.

"Hold on! Ain't nobody going nowhere!" yelled one of the men as he pointed a 9mm straight at Ian.

The skinny man wore a sleeveless gray shirt and dirty, worn-out blue jeans. The other man ran over to the driver's side, opened the door, and pointed a double barrel shotgun at Lynn. He was a little stockier than the first man and wore a red flannel shirt with the sleeves half-rolled up his tattooed arms.

"Get out!" he shouted.

Ian stood still as he looked at the man in front of him watching his partner force Lynn out of the van.

"Whoo boys! A news van!" shouted Ian's aggressor.

Ian tried to bargain with the men. "Look guys, we can take you where you want to go. It doesn't have to be like this."

The man jumped a few steps closer to Ian. "Hey buddy, you just keep your mouth shut if you know what's best!"

Once Lynn got out of the van, the stocky man pointed his shotgun at Sarah and told her to get out as well. Ian nervously watched as she eased toward the driver's side. The man grabbed Sarah by the arm and threw her out of the van onto the asphalt. Ian ran straight to his wife's aide. The man with the pistol chased Ian to the other side as he yelled at him. Just as Ian came around and was about to grab Sarah's attacker, the skinny guy pulled the trigger and shot Ian in the leg. Ian fell to the ground.

Sarah screamed, jumped to her feet, and hurried

over to Ian.

Lynn tried to reason with the men. "Stop, please listen! We need to get that man to Highlands Regional. A doctor at Pikeville Medical Center told us that his blood could find a cure for all of this! We just need to get him over there as soon as possible."

Skeptical, the man with the shotgun looked to his partner. "Look lady, if anybody needs to get to the hospital, it'd be me!" He pulled the top of his shirt down to expose a huge bite mark on his upper chest. "One of them things bit me, and the hospital is where we're fixing to go. Now, get back, or I swear, I'll plow you over with your own van!"

Lynn took a few steps closer to the men. She desperately begged at them. "Please! It's very important that he gets to Dr. Parker! If not, then there's a chance this virus can spread to every single person in the country! Maybe even the world!"

The man moved to get inside the van as he said, "I guess the world's just hurtin' then."

Lynn approached the man with her hands out as she begged him not to leave them there. He pointed his shotgun and fired at her. Lynn fell to the ground as a gush of blood sprayed from her back. Horrified, Sarah screamed as she saw a puddle of blood form under Lynn's body. The man then turned the gun at Sarah and fired another shot directly into her chest. She fell over next to Ian.

Something in Ian’s mind snapped as he looked at Sarah's lifeless body lying on the gray pavement. As the men hurried to get inside the van, Ian no longer felt the pain from the gunshot to his leg. He stood and limped over to the men. The man wearing the sleeveless shirt pointed his pistol out of the window and fired three shots into Ian's chest. The men shouted in victory as Ian fell to his knees. He placed his hand on his bloody uniform shirt and watched as the red stain grew larger and larger. His vision blurred as he gasped for air; his entire body felt numb. At last, his face collided with the road as he fell forward. The van's tires squealed as the men sped away from the bloody mess they'd created. Silence settled in as Ian lay with his eyes open, fixated on Sarah's body. Ian's heart stopped as he took his final breath. The life left his body, and along with it, so did humanity's only chance to survive the zombie apocalypse.

BLACKOUT

Shadows of trees blowing in the wind danced across the walls surrounding Frank. Moonlight beamed down through the branches, pouring over his small dome tent and onto the forest floor. Frank fell asleep after having a large dinner he cooked over the campfire. The fire had died out and only a small flame flickered amongst the glowing embers. Before lying down, Frank knew the mountain air would get colder throughout the night, so he put on a red beanie over his shaggy, auburn hair. He wore thick clothes all over his tall, slender body and cocooned himself inside a green sleeping bag.

Frank's life had been rough. He lost his job, and no one wanted to hire him. Before the phone company disconnected him, bill collectors called every day asking for the late payments on his mortgage and medical bills. About to lose everything, Frank decided he needed to get away for a few days before he went insane. Frank always found camping to be a great way to escape.

The air felt calm with an occasional gentle breeze whistling through the woods. Crickets sang a lullaby to every living creature in the forest. All at once, the stillness was shattered as a bloodcurdling scream came from deep within the woods. Frank immediately awoke. Confused, he lay still and listened. Another terrified shriek pierced the silence. Startled, Frank's body jerked. He raised his head and looked around while trying to process everything. He thought no one else would be around him for miles that far out in the woods.

"Help me!" screamed the female voice.

Frank's eyes frantically moved side-to-side as the nylon walls of the tent moved in and out, being pushed around by the wind, almost resembling Frank's panicked breaths. His heart fluttered.

"Please, somebody! He's after me! He killed my family!" yelled the woman. Her voice moved closer to the campsite, and the distress in her voice sent chills down Frank's spine.

Frank contemplated what really happened to the woman and if he should help. Fear of the unknown paralyzed him inside the sleeping bag. His mind began to weave possible scenarios of what might happen if he went outside. A pistol sat tucked away in Frank's red backpack on the other side of the tent. Frank rose up in the sleeping bag when the woman let out another high-pitched shriek. He continued to struggle with himself about whether to help the woman or stay there in his tent and hope to go unnoticed. He lay still and listened as the helpless cries faded into the distance.

Frank felt his heart was about to pound out of his chest. Too afraid to go back to sleep, Frank's mind raced, and he'd never felt more afraid of being alone in all of his life. After lying in silence for at least an hour, Frank's eyelids became heavy as he tried to fight fatigue. Frank's body finally gave into its urge to rest; he fell back to sleep.

Frank awoke the next morning to a rumble of thunder. The mountains seemed as peaceful as ever. He rose up from the ground while trying to focus his thoughts and remember if the woman screaming in the woods was real or just a bad dream. He realized there was indeed someone in the woods with him during the night. A sense of guilt came over Frank as he grasped the fact that the woman was screaming for help, and he did nothing to help her. Frank began to suspect the killer may still be in the woods with him. He made a quick decision to leave the tent and sleeping bag there. He jumped up and grabbed the red backpack sitting in the corner. All he cared about was getting out of the woods before the killer found him. As the backpack hung on his left shoulder, he unzipped the tent door and glanced around the camp. The woods looked empty. Frank didn't bother zipping the door back as he stepped out and set off toward his truck parked next to the road a few miles away.

An unsettling scream burst out of the silence. Frank stopped in his tracks immediately. It sounded like another woman and came from an area close by. A boy began wailing in the distance as well. Both voices came from the same direction. Frank wanted to get back to his truck and go home, but he knew he would regret that decision for the rest of his days. Hesitant, Frank knelt down, put the backpack on the ground, and unzipped it. He retrieved the black 9mm pistol from inside and slid the pack over his shoulders. He started toward the screams.

Frank checked the gun chamber to make sure a round was ready to fire. He stepped lightly through the woods that surrounded him. Frank could tell the voices came from just ahead as he passed a towering oak tree. Then as suddenly as the screams began, they stopped. Frank felt the hair on the back of his neck stand up.

Something seemed wrong.

He continued toward the direction of the screaming and soon found himself walking into a field. Frank looked around for any sign of life. He spotted three strange mounds of earth aligned in a straight row. As Frank carefully approached the mounds, he noticed a medium-sized sandstone rock standing at the back of each of them. The strange bulges of earth looked fresh; Frank suspected they weren't made long before. He pulled the tight collar of his sweater away from his throat. Oddly, there was a half-dug hole next to the three mounds.

Frank nearly jumped out of his skin when he felt a cold wind blow against his ear as an old man whispered, "Please, don't hurt her!"

Scared out of his wits, Frank turned and ran toward his truck. He heard the sounds of heavy footsteps chasing him away from the field. After Frank ran for a good distance, he turned to catch a glimpse of his pursuer, but no one was there. When Frank noticed the footsteps had disappeared, he slowed down to a jog. Out of breath, Frank leaned against a tree to rest for a moment. His chest pounded and sweat poured from his body. Frank jerked the red beanie off his head and ran his fingers through his wet, mangled hair. He leaned his head against the moss covered bark on the tree. A sudden high-pitched scream came from the opposite side of the tall oak

Frank leaned against. He jumped forward and looked to the other side.

As he backed away, the voice of a young boy whispered, “Mom! Dad!”

Frank turned. The female voice screamed relentlessly and seemed to surround him. Frank stepped backwards as he frantically looked around the forest for the sources of the voices. Frank saw no one. His head twisted back and forth; his breaths, short and quick. Frank felt the back of his foot hit something. He lost his balance and fell to the forest floor, striking his head against a large rock. Frank’s vision started to blur as the screams faded away. Just as everything started to go black, Frank saw three figures surround him. He barely made out the distinct silhouettes of an older man, woman, and a young boy.

***

“Hey, Scotty! I found him over here!” yelled a man shining a flashlight on Frank.

Frank struggled to open his eyes. He heard dogs barking in the distance and footfalls rapidly crunching the fallen leaves.

“Frank! Are you okay?”

Frank felt dizzy and had a dull pain in the back of his head. He raised his head to see the man. Another man came running through the woods toward Frank; he wore a dark jacket with reflective strips

The man wearing the jacket held a two-way radio up to his mouth and said, “Chief, this is Scotty. We found him. Send somebody with a stretcher up here. We’re about a quarter-mile northeast from the truck.” Scotty walked over to the other man who knelt down beside Frank. “Jack, is he responding?”

"He's awake."

"Frank, can you hear me?" asked Scotty.

Frank blinked his eyes a few times. "Yes. What's going on?"

"Just lay still. It looks like you've hit your head pretty hard."

Frank remembered the three people standing above him as he blacked out. "Where are they?"

"Help's on the way, Frank," said Jack.

"No! There were three of them! They chased me out here!"

"Easy, Frank. Who are you talking about?"

"Somebody was trying to kill them! Then, they came after me! I was afraid to help them!"

Jack looked up at Scotty with his eyebrows raised. "Scotty, you don't think he's talking about—"

"Jack!" Scotty interrupted. "Frank, do you remember anything about last night?"

With wide eyes, Frank said, "A young woman was screaming, saying somebody was after her in the woods. I was too afraid to do anything about it so I stayed in my tent. I should have gone out to help, but I didn't!"

With a stern, almost angry look, Scotty said, "Frank, you've had another one of your spells."

Frank's mouth hung open. He glanced at both men. "Spell?"

"He doesn't remember, Scotty. He never does."

"What are you talking about?" demanded Frank.

Scotty let out a sigh. "Frank, you really don't remember anything?"

"Yes! I told you!"

Scotty turned and walked a few feet away.

Jack shook his head. "Frank, you have D.I.D.: Dissociative Identity Disorder. You have blackout spells, and you can't remember what happens when you're not yourself. The spells usually make you have amnesia afterwards. They should've never let you out in the first place."

"What does all that mean? What about those people who were after me?"

Scotty turned and yelled, "You killed them, Frank!"

Numbness came over Frank as he realized what he had done. "But that girl, she needed my help!"

"That girl was running from you. She got away and ran to the road where somebody picked her up last night," Jack told him.

Scotty added, "Now that poor girl is going to have to go through the rest of her life without her parents and brother!"

Frank started crying as he lay there on the forest floor. Soon, two other rescue workers ran to Frank with the stretcher. The four men put Frank on the stretcher and carried him out of the forest. A tow truck sat in front of Frank's truck as they brought him to the ambulance parked beside the road. The paramedics loaded Frank onto a gurney and up into the ambulance. As the rescue team shut the doors, Frank watched the tow truck pull away with his truck behind it. He closed his eyes and sobbed as the ambulance started along its way to the hospital, thirty minutes away.

Frank woke up in a hospital room strapped to a bed. He couldn't remember much about the ride there in the ambulance. He began to overhear a conversation between two nurses who stood outside his door, discussing the horrible ambulance wreck Frank was involved in.

"They said he killed all of them except the driver

right before the ambulance crashed into the creek."

THE HUNGRIEST ZOMBIE

Ed doesn't like sitting around much these days. In fact, his favorite brown penny loafers are starting to show signs of heavy travel. Not that Ed enjoys walking the seemingly empty streets of Morristown; he does it only out of necessity. There isn't much to be said of anything he does enjoy anymore.

The sun is hanging high in the blue summer sky. Its scorching rays beaming straight atop Ed's bald, liver-spotted head. He is an older man, not a day younger than seventy at the least. He's dressed to kill in his tattered button-up green and white plaid shirt, half tucked into his dark blue slacks. As Ed staggers around the cars that are lining the street in a careless jumble, random pieces of paper and garbage waft by his slender body. Each vehicle is abandoned, much like the buildings surrounding them. Ed doesn't mind the death and destruction around him in this small Tennessee town. Truthfully, he couldn't care less about the events that have brought his hometown to this lowly state.

Several months ago, Morristown was a thriving place, growing with each year that passed. Being a stubborn old man, Ed was always wary of the changes going on around him. The same was to be said when the Great Plague reached his town. Friends and family tried to reason and convince Ed to come to one of the national safe houses set up by the government after the outbreak reached mass hysteria; he didn't listen. Ed thought he would be safe at his home with his trusty old Winchester rifle. He made a grave mistake. He thought his ammo would last him until the government had the mess cleaned up, but it didn't.

With all that was happening outside, sleep was scarce for him during that time. One evening, Ed was at his normal post; sitting in his rocking chair on his front porch, holding his Winchester on his lap. He was feeling the effects of countless sleepless nights weighing his eyes shut. A howl from one of the creatures startled Ed from his sleep. He tried to react as it ran toward him, but the 'click' of a vacant chamber was all that came from his gun. While leaning over for more bullets, he was surprised to find an empty box sitting beside him.

The zombie was on him before he could think of another plan, and Ed was dead. It didn't finish devouring Ed's body; passers-by distracted the monster as they ran across the street to help Ed. They couldn't help. Ed may have been only partially eaten, but he was still dead and infected.

Now, Ed is here. He's one of the lucky ones. Others are living and fighting the inevitable. Morristown is overrun by the living dead. At times, screams and the occasional burst of gunfire snatches Ed's attention, but right now, nothing can tear him away from what lies before him. A man is lying on the sweltering pavement, dead. His body was half-eaten by the marauding hoards of flesh-hungry beasts that rule this town. He hasn't been dead for very long. His blood–still oozing from his wounds–is warm, and only a few flies have begun their own feast on his lifeless corpse.

He was left half-dead by his attackers, whose attention was drawn by a survivor in the man's group. The survivor followed the man's cries for help which led to his own demise.

Ed staggers with each step. His eyes, blotched with red around the whites of his greenish-grey irises, are fixated on the mangled mound of flesh and bones lying there in the scorching heat. His mouth opens wide as a snarling hiss comes from within the depths of his throat. His boney hands begin to reach outward toward the body. The skin on his hands is nearly transparent as dark veins bulge from beneath. Large chunks missing from his skin leave huge open wounds all over his body. Slowly, he approaches the rotting carcass in hopes of feeding his insatiable zombie hunger.

Finally, Ed's staggering march comes to a stop as he falls to his knees beside the body of the fallen man. Ed leans over; his arms, head, and torso are all jerking uncontrollably. His mouth opens wider. Incoherent moans seem to just fall from his throat with each inch that he moves closer to his feast of putrid human remains.

His dry, blue lips at last meet an undisturbed section of skin left over from the last patrons. His protruding jaws begin to gnaw. With each chomp Ed increases the pressure of his bite, but nothing is working. He is growing frustrated with each attack on the skin, trying desperately to tear away the skin and muscle attached to the bones. Frantically, Ed tries to bite off any morsel that will rip from the man's corpse. Nothing is happening.

In a fit of rage, Ed turns his crooked head toward the sky, and with his decaying fists held in a tight clinch thrust skyward, he lets out a tormented roar for all to hear. Ed has no teeth. He lost them many years ago to the gum disease gingivitis. This is now his curse, to wander the earth mindlessly in search of the only thing to sooth his hunger: the warm, meaty flesh of humans. Yet, without his teeth to tear through skin, Ed is merely half the zombie he could be.

Normally zombies are emotionless creatures, but Ed's torture is so great that he has slowly begun to feel resentment for his toothless condition. Attracted by his agonizing cry, a small horde of zombies come to feast on Ed's fresh find, and unfortunately, Ed finds himself outside the crowd of mindless monsters. The scene resembles that of a litter of puppies nudging their way to their mother's milk as the runt of the litter is pushed aside by its brothers and sisters. Ed tries to make his way back into the huddle with disappointing results. On his hands and knees he scurries around all the others, but there's no space between the devouring zombies.

He looks across the mob and gazes at each face for a moment. Ed notices the mangled, rotten teeth in some of their mouths; most are chipped and discolored. Others are nice, undamaged, and covered in the blood of Ed's discovery. A few of these animals seem almost boastful in the way they have bitten off their lips during the madness to fulfill their need to feed.

Soon, the horde slowly breaks away to reveal a

mound of bones. Looking at the pile as the others limp away to their next meal, Ed groans with frustration. A few grape-sized meaty chunks lay on the ground, overlooked by the others. Ed reaches over to pick them up and puts them into his mouth. He gums the pieces as hard and fast as he can. The juices and taste of human flesh only tease Ed further. With one gulp, his meal is over.

Staggering, he struggles to get to his feet. With yet another groan, Ed begins his staggering walk in search of his next meal. At the end of the street stands a large building–the hospital. The mammoth building holds a look of promise as he slowly walks through the middle of the street toward it.

All around him humans and zombies are at war with one another. On the sidewalk to his left, a group of zombies tackle a screaming young woman. Behind him Ed can hear guns being fired and a man yelling for help. Everywhere, mayhem grips the city. However, Ed is oblivious to it all; his sights are set solely on the hospital.

Arriving at the hospital entrance, the automatic doors aren't functioning–the electricity has been knocked out for months now. The glass has been broken out of the doors. Ed struggles to lift his foot over the bottom of the left doorway as he makes his way into the building. Clumsily, he trips over it and plunges face-first to the ground, covering himself with small beads of broken glass. The small shards embed into Ed's skin, causing his black, decomposed blood to ooze from his wounds. Unfazed, Ed struggles to his feet again. He pauses to look around for a moment. The lobby is in shambles. Furniture is overturned everywhere, and the door leading to the gift shop has been broken down by looters during the first wave of panic. The dim blue light coming from the wall of tinted windows floods the granite tile floor. Ed begins moving down the dark hallway to his left. A few beams of light trickle through open doorways–coming from windows inside the rooms–spilling out onto small portions of the hallway.

Ed slowly creeps down the long hall, occasionally bumping into beds, wheelchairs, and other supplies left in a cluttered mess by frightened employees. Ed is hungry. With each second that passes, the need inside of him grows. Leftovers just aren't adequate anymore. He needs a meal–a warm, fresh meal.

The sound of something hitting the floor disrupts the ominous silence. Ed's eyes search the corridor as he stands still for a moment. His primal instinct kicks in, and he is now on the hunt. Attentively, he listens for the slightest sound. Moments pass by with nothing. The calmness settles back in. Silence once again fills the empty halls.

Ed lets out a modest groan as he turns his head to look around. His movements are stuttered and awkward. His twisted head turns, his mouth open. Every now and then, a soft moan makes its way from his throat. His distorted hands are limp as he holds one forearm to his stomach and his other arm bent slightly outward. His stance is to some extent crouched, or merely hunched over. Ed begins slowly creeping forward with his head turned to the side to hear from either behind or in front of him. With each step, his anticipation grows.

As he comes closer to the end of the hall, a faint commotion can be heard just around the corner. His pace quickens. A light is moving around, making shadows dance across the papered walls. Ed finally reaches the hall's end. He looks around the corner in anticipation. A man about the same age as Ed is standing there. He is wearing a dirty, plain grey t-shirt with small holes ripped in it. His khaki pants are stained with blood and dirt. His hair is grey and uncombed. The man looks beaten and broken by time and exhaustion.

Frantically, the man is gathering various medical supplies from a small closet and putting them into an old, green Army duffel bag. Obviously nervous, his hands are quivering as he grabs bandages and ointments.

Ed's eyes grow wider, and he lets out a wretched wail as he hastily staggers after his prey. Horrified, the man ditches everything he has gathered as he drops back from his position. He is unaware of Ed's condition. His eyes are lit up with fear as he reaches in his pocket for his radio.

He holds it to his mouth and yells, "I'm in trouble guys! One of them's after me!"

Ed desperately tries to keep up with the man, pushing beds and anything else in his path out of the way. The man turns and begins to sprint away from Ed, trying to put some distance between them. He's tugging at his side, desperate to draw his pistol from its holster. Ed lets out yet another deafening howl as he continues his reckless pursuit. The man is trembling in fear for his life. He has seen these monsters attack and slaughter many others. He saw the horrifying death that came to all the other victims as they screamed in terror and anguish as the zombies chewed at their bodies until their breath was gone.

The old man can't run very fast; he's pushing his body to its limits, trying to allow himself enough time to draw his weapon. He makes his way through the dark corridor, unsure of where he is going as he glances down at his sidearm, all the while, his pursuer is still heavy on his trail. At last, the man manages to free his gun. He makes a quick turn and points it toward Ed, who is still coming full speed toward the man. With unsteady hands, he pulls the trigger. A burst of fire comes from the barrel and lights up the dark passage for a split second. The shot misses. Ed is heedless to the danger he is facing; his only concern is to feed.

He continues his mad dash toward the man. Another shot is fired, but it merely grazes Ed's shoulder. Blood oozes from the wound, and the impact causes Ed's torso to jerk violently. This slows Ed's momentum for only a couple of seconds before he resumes his pursuit. Ed lets out an enraged screech as he hobbles after the old man. Hearing this, the man turns and once again continues running from Ed. Looking back, he turns the gun toward Ed one last time. A sound far more petrifying than the blood-curdling shrills of the undead comes from his gun: click. The man has run out of bullets. Panic overcomes him. A flood of terror rushes through his body.

"Help me! Somebody, please! Help!" screams the man.

Tears begin to fall from his eyes. The two run through the dark passageway leading to another foyer. The man is out of breath; he struggles to fill his lungs with air. He clutches his chest as a searing pain rushes through it. His stride comes to an abrupt halt as he falls to the floor. Ed seizes the opportunity as the man lays there twitching and gasping for air. He leaps onto his victim and begins gnawing impenetrably at the man's neck.

The man now lays lifeless, his heart has given out.

Ed is determined that he is going to make a meal of the man.

But just as all the times before, Ed finds himself in a no-win situation. Nothing he does will work, no matter how hard he bites. Feverishly he tries the arms, legs, and stomach, but nothing. Ed grabs the man by his shirt, and out of desperation, begins howling and violently shaking the man's lifeless body. His arms flop about. His head freely bobs up and down repeatedly hitting the floor. Blood splatters and pours from the back of the man's head.

Surprisingly, something comes out of the man's mouth landing alongside the body. Ed stops for a moment to see what the item is. It's in two pieces, pink, and looks very strange, unlike anything Ed has seen before.

He releases his grip on the man and cautiously leans over to observe these foreign objects. Confused, he reaches his trembling hands toward the objects. Upon first touch, the items are wet with saliva. Ed recognizes them and soon realizes what he is holding: teeth. The man's dentures were jarred loose when Ed was hitting his head against the floor. He lets out a puzzled moan as he examines the teeth.

Ed tries scratching and tapping their surface with his encrusted fingernails. He just can't understand.

Out of some partial instinct, he holds the dentures in the correct fashion, but struggles with unsteady hands and head as he awkwardly slides them into his mouth. Some remnant of denture cream still covers them and creates a solid bond to his gums. He bites together and feels something he has never felt in his entire zombie life. Ed now has teeth.

As Ed once again leans over the man's body, it seems almost as if he is smiling. The first bite takes a little effort to puncture the skin, but nonetheless, the pleasing taste of blood and flesh soon floods his mouth. His chewing is a little sloppy at first. He pushes the generous portions of meat around in his mouth with his tongue, trying to hold it within the grip of his new teeth.

Soon, Ed is getting mouthfuls of meat as he rips cartilage from the bones. Surprisingly, the denture cream is holding quite nicely. Ed is so spellbound by his meal he doesn't notice the large muscular man with an AK-47 running toward him. He is sporting a white tank top with camouflage pants, dressed for war from his head to his black combat boots.

The man stops several feet from Ed and with a look of discontent, puts his two-way radio to his mouth and says in a deep voice, "They killed Bruce!"

Ed stops immediately to look up. Seeing the man, Ed hesitates for a moment between finishing his meal, which he has only taken a few bites of, or landing a fresh kill. Ed snarls and lets out a ghastly hiss at the man. The man squints his eyes and points his gun at Ed.

"Die, scumbag," the man says calmly as he fires a quick burst of ammo straight into Ed's forehead.

Instantly, Ed's body jerks as he falls backward to the floor. The man waits for a moment. He lowers his gun, then turns and walks back down the hall. As Ed lies next to Bruce, the silence and loneliness settles back in. The force that once controlled Ed's body has left. Along with it, the man has managed to rid Ed of his constant problem: he has cured Ed's hunger.

THE MOTHMAN ISN'T REAL

"Man, I just can't catch a break," said Darryl as he reeled the lure back to the boat after yet another Houdini fish got away.

"I don't think either of us is catching much of anything today," laughed Sam. He planned this rare fishing trip for his best friend in good faith.

Darryl reeled the chartreuse spinner bait up from the calm, green water. Nervously, he checked his watch. Darryl knew if he failed to meet Ann's expectations once again, she wouldn't be happy. It had been the same throughout their eight-year marriage, and Darryl always tried hard not to disappoint his wife. Reluctant, he once again cast the lure near a submerged fallen pine. As his spinner bait fell toward the water, a sparkle of sunlight danced across its shiny metal blades. The day faded away as evening settled in. The sun sat behind the mountaintop and the sky wore a blend of deep oranges and light purples.

"God, it's beautiful out here," commented Sam as

he looked to the sky. "Remember when we were in grade school and our moms nearly had to beat us with a stick to get us back inside?"

Darryl nodded as he too looked up. "Yeah, those were the days. You know, we really had it made back then. No worries, just carefree days of playing outside."

Darryl and Sam had been friends since the second grade. Throughout their twenty year friendship, Sam never saw Darryl this way until he and Ann got together. Things started slowly between Darryl and Ann, but the longer the two were together, the more controlling Ann became. Darryl knew this himself, but never found the courage to admit it, much less to leave.

"Hey, I like to think I still live that way," said Sam. He was in a few relationships, but never anything serious.

Darryl laughed. "Yeah, you do! I'd have to say, you're a prime example of a bachelor, my friend."

Sam chuckled and said, "You say that like it's a bad thing."

Darryl watched his lure splash along the water's surface as he replied, "No, there's nothing wrong with that at all. You've got it made, man! You can do what you want. You can buy anything you want without having to worry about somebody always telling you what a waste of money it was." Darryl shook his head as he cast his lure back into the lake. "I'd trade places with you in a heartbeat."

Sam turned on the trolley motor with its foot pedal. He guided the boat a little further down the shoreline.

"Let me ask you a question, Darryl." Sam's tone seemed more serious. "What's stopping you from having all of that?"

Darryl cast toward some rocks along the shore. "I'm married. That's all over for me," he said with a sheepish laugh.

Sam stopped the trolley motor and cast his lure. "It don't have to be that way though, Darryl. Yeah sure you're married, but things don't have to be the way they are between you and Ann. You guys don't even have kids."

Darryl hesitated as he said, "Well, I love her. She loves me too. She just likes to have things her way, sometimes. I just let her have it; it's easier that way." Darryl was very uncomfortable talking that way. He hated making excuses for Ann.

"Yeah, yeah." Sam grinned. "How did you talk her into letting you come out here today?"

Darryl tried to be firm as he said, "I told her we were planning this for a while."

Sam's eyebrows rose. "How'd that go over?"

Darryl shook his head. He felt a knot form in his throat. "Not so well. We had a really big argument before I left. I still feel kinda bad about the stuff I said." Darryl held in a lot of emotions. He stood uneasy at the back of the boat and hoped Sam changed the subject soon.

"Ah, don't worry about it, buddy." Sam looked up at the sky. "I believe the fish have all gone to sleep or something. I'd say it's about time to head back to the dock."

Relieved, Darryl hurried to reel in his bait. "Yeah, it's starting to get dark out."

The two men put away their poles and put their lifejackets on. Darryl sat down in the passenger seat as Sam lifted the trolley motor out of the lake and folded it down into place.

"Ah, even if we didn't catch anything, it was still good to get out like this again," said Sam while he sat down in the driver's seat.

Darryl stared straight ahead as he replied, "Yeah, it was."

Sam turned the key in the ignition; the motor struggled to turn over. After a moment, Sam let off and tried it again. The engine wouldn't start. Darryl chuckled to himself.

Sam smacked his hand against the steering wheel and said, "This stupid thing. I just had it worked on last week!"

"Why didn't you just buy a new boat or at least a new motor? This one is shot," laughed Darryl.

Sam declared, "I got a good deal on this baby."

"A good deal?" Darryl laughed even more. "You got took on that deal. I know you could've afforded to buy a brand new one for what you spent to get this worked on."

"Yeah, but I guess you live and you learn. Good thing I did spring on the new battery for the trolley motor." Sam walked to the front and put the trolley motor back in to the water. "Looks like we're gonna have a long ride home tonight."

Darryl smiled and took the lifejacket back off. He pulled his cell phone out of his pocket to call Ann. "Crap, no signal." They were deep in the narrow backwaters of Fishtrap Lake. It was the closest lake around their hometown, Pikeville, KY. They knew the lake like the back of their hands, and there had always been much better fishing in the backwaters. But surrounded by the tall wooded mountains, the modern convenience of cell phone service seemed hard to come by.

Soon the sun sank completely out of sight, and the

moon rose above the mountains. The sky darkened, and the burning lights of a thousand stars hung suspended above the two friends. Sam's rugged boat buzzed along the water under the beautiful night sky. Darryl held a spotlight for Sam to see the way.

"This sucks," said Sam.

"You'll learn next time, now, won't you?" asked Darryl as he once again laughed at Sam's frugalness. He checked his cell phone again, still no signal. They traveled for about an hour and a half, but only made it a short distance. With the trolley motor maxed out, it pulled them across the lake at a rate of about a foot per second. Calmness filled the air. An owl hooted in the trees up ahead.

"At least we've got a full moon out tonight," said Sam, trying to make light of the situation.

The two looked at the moon. Its light shone down and dimly lit everything around them. As they looked back toward the front of the boat, something big flew over them, blocking the moon's light above them for just a second.

"What the heck was that?" asked Sam.

All of a sudden, the loud sounds of snapping twigs and rustling leaves came from the treetops just down the narrow lake. As quickly as it started, it stopped. Darryl shined the spotlight on the treetops along the shore. The light moved across the mountain as they continued to search for the source of the commotion. Something caught Darryl's eye in a tall birch tree. He moved the light back to the tree. Surprised, Darryl and Sam saw a large gray object. As they strained to get a better view, the creature suddenly turned its head to reveal two bright, glowing red eyes reflected in the light. It held an owl's bloody body in its hands. Terrified by the sight of the creature, Darryl and Sam flinched. All at once the creature squinted its eyes and let out a wretched screech. It spread its massive wings, and with one mighty swoop, it took off straight into the sky.

Horrified, Darryl asked, “What was that thing?”

“I don’t know, but it didn’t look too happy! Try to start the motor again; we need to get out of here!”

Darryl jumped down into the driver’s seat and cranked the motor. It wouldn’t start. The light from the moon overhead faded away once again for a second. Sam jumped up from the seat and ran to the back. He started messing with the gas line to the motor. The men heard the creature’s wings flapping as it circled above them.

Distressed, Sam said, “Try it now!”

Darryl turned the key once more. The engine roared as it started. Without hesitation, Darryl pushed the throttle forward.

“Shine me a light!” yelled Darryl to Sam.

Sam sat down in the seat next to Darryl as he fumbled for the spotlight. He found it lying in the floor and shined it out over the boat’s bow. Darryl drove the beat-up boat through the winding waterway at top speed. After a moment, they heard the same screeching sound from earlier. They both turned as Sam directed the light to the stern. A wave of terror came over them when they saw the creature flying right behind them. They found it impossible to make out any facial features due to the bright red light reflecting from its eyes. Its massive wings flapped as it flew close to the lake’s surface; the water beneath it pitched about. Its wings spread out twice the width of the boat on each side.

Sam hurried to a compartment at the front of the boat.

"What are you doing?" asked Darryl.

Sam rummaged through the compartment for a moment and pulled out a flare gun.

"I'm gonna burn that thing!" yelled Sam.

He pointed the gun at the beast and fired. The bright fireball made direct contact, and the monster flipped backwards into the lake. Excited, Darryl and Sam yelled in victory.

"Let's get home!" said Sam as he continued to let Darryl drive his pride and joy.

Seconds later, the motor began sputtering. Sam hurried to the back and fidgeted with the gas line again. The boat lost speed as Sam nervously checked all of the hoses and wires. The engine smoked and gave out. They floated along for a moment as Darryl tried to start the engine again. Between engine cranks, they heard the flapping sound return.

"Reach me the light!" said Sam. Darryl leaned over to grab the light when a long shadow blocked the moonlight.

"It's coming back!" yelled Darryl as he looked up.

"I'm gonna knock it out of the sky this time!" Sam went to the side of the boat, opened a storage compartment, and got out a large wooden paddle. "Shine the light for me, Darryl."

As Darryl pointed the light, the creature turned, swooped down, and headed straight toward them. Its eyes glowed in the light as it let out a deafening screech. It made a quick pass by the boat as Sam swung with all of his might. He barely missed the monster as it flew past them. Darryl watched as it glided around and started toward them again. Sam readied the paddle once more as the creature approached. With another deafening howl, the creature lowered its muscular arms. It flew just above the water as it approached them. All of a sudden, the mighty creature grabbed the back of the boat with its hands and flipped it over on its top. The boat and everything in it made a huge splash.

Darryl tried to make his way back up to the surface. He still held the spotlight in his hand. Darryl gasped for air as he came up and looked around.

"Sam!" he screamed. "Sam, where are you?"

There was no reply.

He tried to shine the spotlight, but it barely flickered on, which made it hard to see anything. Silence filled the air, and Darryl feared the worst. He continued to yell for Sam until he heard the creature swoop above him. Scared and alone, he turned off the light and swam quietly to the shore. The beast let out another screech as it circled in the sky.

Once Darryl reached the shore, he tried to stand with unsteady knees. His entire body trembled in fear. Darryl stumbled for a moment and managed to make it a few feet. Clouds moved in and blocked the light of the moon. Darryl had a tough time seeing where he went. He bumped the spotlight against a tree on accident. The light flashed on for a moment. The creature saw the light and flew down to the shore. Darryl threw the spotlight in the opposite direction in an attempt to distract the monster. He turned and ran up the mountain, through the woods.

The creature landed where the light did, but realized its prey had fled. It soon gave chase to Darryl.

Darryl heard the monster running up the hill after him. He pulled the phone from his drenched pocket and pressed every button in hopes that the phone might work. After Darryl deemed his efforts useless, he turned and threw the phone at the persistent creature.

At last the clouds gave way, moonlight flooded through the treetops onto the forest floor. Darryl looked for the monster. It was nowhere in sight, but he heard its footsteps just down the hill. He looked for a safe place to hide. To his left, he noticed a large fallen tree just beyond a huge thicket of brier bushes. At the base of the tree stood a massive root ball, the dirt and roots made a wall twice as tall as Darryl. He dove to the ground and crawled underneath the thicket. Darryl moved as fast as his body allowed; using elbows and knees to push through the briers. The sharp thorns tore into Darryl's skin. Cuts soon covered his body, but the adrenaline pumping through it numbed every bit of the pain.

At last, Darryl managed to make it out of the thicket. He scurried on hands and knees behind the root ball. Darryl sat and pressed his back against the roots and dirt. He fought his lungs, trying to silence the heavy breaths.

The monster arrived just on the other side of the thicket. Darryl heard its steps come to a stop. The creature breathed heavily as it stood still to listen and watch for Darryl. Fear consumed Darryl. All he seemed to think about was his wife and the fight they had before he'd left.

The monster took a few steps closer to Darryl. He tried to calm himself with the thought that the creature may not come through the thicket to look for him. He heard its footsteps as it crept around his thorn fortress. Soon, the creature stood directly to his left–just feet away. Darryl moved only his eyes to watch the monster. Its posture had a slight hunch, yet it still stood at least an enormous nine-feet-tall from the top of its folded wings to its massive clawed feet. Even without the wings, it measured well over seven feet from head to toe. Its skin was gray and leathery. The moonlight revealed its muscular physique. The creature twitched its elongated fingers where long black claws protruded from the tips. Darryl struggled to make out any of the creature's facial features. He observed it didn't have a nose visible from the side. It seemed as though, if any light at all was present, its eyes reflected it. The soft moonlight made the glowing eyes less intense than the spotlight did.

The beast stood there moving its head as it hunted for Darryl. Darryl anticipated the mammoth beast might spot him soon. He glanced on the forest floor around him. He saw a thick branch, that had previously broken off the pine tree, laid within reaching distance from where he sat. Darryl glanced back at the creature; it stared at a small pile of rocks just in front of Darryl. He felt for the stick with his fingertips as he kept a close eye on the creature. It moved its head around and appeared it was within inches of making eye contact with Darryl. He felt the rough bark of his intended weapon and grasped it tightly in his hand. He held still and prepared for the moment when the creature spotted him.

Without warning, a bright light came tearing through the dense foliage from the lake below. Voices yelled Darryl's name. Startled, the creature turned around toward the light. It unfolded its enormous wings and leapt into the air. Darryl watched as the creature flapped its wings and flew off toward the top of the mountain. A sudden rush of relief came over him; he hurried to crawl out of the thicket. Once out, he rose to his feet and ran down through the trees and other vegetation. The light bounced around the woods, and the voices grew louder. He recognized one of the voices–Sam. Darryl felt even more relieved to hear his voice. Two unfamiliar voices also called for Darryl.

Once he got closer to the lake he yelled, "I'm here!"

The voices stopped for a second and yelled back, "Where are you?"

The moment he reached the water, Darryl jumped in. He saw a game warden's boat with flashing blue lights beside Sam's capsized boat. The spotlight pinpointed on Darryl.

Sam yelled, "There he is!"

As Darryl swam, someone threw him a life preserver and pulled him to the boat. One game warden with a thick gray mustache reached his hand down. Darryl noticed the man's name, James, on a shiny gold nametag on his shirt. Darryl stretched his hand up to grab James'. Another game warden rushed over to grab Darryl's other hand. The other man looked at least twenty years younger than James, his face was clean-shaven; his name was Steve. Both men pulled Darryl up out of the water and into the boat. Sam stood there next to them; his head was bandaged. He reached over and hugged Darryl.

Darryl looked at Sam and asked, "Did you tell them already?"

Sam wore a disgusted look on his face and said, "Yeah."

With a smirk across his face, Steve said, "Your buddy here told us about Mothman turning his boat over." Steve and James looked at each other and laughed.

Darryl became very frustrated with the men, "Look buddy, we're not lying!"

James held his hands up and replied, "Okay, calm

down. Just kidding around." He paused before he asked, "You boys been drinking or anything tonight?"

"No!" Darryl firmly stated.

"Well you're gonna have to fill out a report for us about your wreck," said Steve as he crossed his arms.

Darryl looked at Sam, who peered over at his wrecked boat as he agreed.

James went to the back of the boat and unraveled a large rope. He walked to the front and asked Darryl and Sam to have a seat while he and Steve hooked up to Sam's boat; they needed to tow it back to the dock. Darryl and Sam sat down as the men connected the boats together. Efficiently, James and Steve had the rope in place. James walked over to the steering wheel and started the engine. Steve stood beside James as he throttled the engine.

The ride back seemed like it took an eternity. Darryl and Sam sat motionless, still in shock over their meeting with the Mothman. Even with his close encounter, Darryl still worried about the fit Ann would have when he got home. The vessel rounded the last curve to the dock. Flashing blue lights came from the parking lot. Darryl stretched his neck to see what happened. James looked over and saw Darryl looking at the lights and said,

"Those lights are for you, son. The police are always involved when it comes to wrecks."

Darryl was puzzled, "Why do they need to be involved?"

James looked toward the lights as he said, "Well, they're gonna need to do some tests on you boys. It's just something they want to do to keep drunks off the lake."

Darryl slumped down in his seat as he muttered, "Great." He knew this would put a longer delay on him going home to an already furious Ann.

The boat floated to a stop beside the dock. All of the men got off and walked up the long walkway to the parking lot. A woman stepped toward them; she was tall and wore a police uniform. The officer greeted James and Steve.

"Well, look who it is! How have you guys been?"

James smiled as he said, "It's been going good, Macy, how about you?"

Macy had her hands on her hips as she looked Darryl and Sam over. "Can't complain. You boys had a pretty bad wreck, I heard."

Sam replied with regret, "Yeah. We're all right, though, so that's all that matters."

Macy looked at Darryl and Sam, as if she examined every move and expression they made. "That's the truth. Well you boys are gonna have to come back to the station with me to take a few tests."

Darryl and Sam followed Macy to her cruiser and got in the back. She drove them to the police station about thirty minutes away. Once there, Darryl asked Macy if there was any way he could use the phone to make a quick call home. Macy explained their policy that anyone brought in was prohibited do anything until their tests were complete. Darryl felt on the verge of having a panic attack. He'd seen Ann mad before over the smallest things, but he knew this time would be the worst.

They underwent breath and blood tests. Once they completed their tests and filled out a report, Macy allowed Darryl to make a phone call. As he approached the black and silver phone that hung on the wall, he felt his chest tighten. Nervous, Darryl dialed the numbers and listened to the rings. After the fourth ring, he knew something must be wrong. Any time he called before, Ann always answered by at least the third ring. The phone rang for the ninth time; Darryl felt his heart sink. He eased the receiver away from his ear and placed it back on the hook. After gathering himself for a moment, he decided to call Ann's cell phone. He grabbed the receiver back off the hook and pecked the numbers.

He pressed the earpiece to his ear and heard a message being played,

"The wireless number you are calling is out of the service area or is turned off."

Ann never set up her voice mail because she always had her phone with her, but it was never off. Darryl feared his wife left him that night. She threatened to leave him before, and for reasons far less than him staying out all night with the best friend she despised.

Darryl walked back to the room where Sam still sat.

Sam looked up at Darryl. "You get a hold of her?"

Darryl walked over to the chair beside him. As he turned to sit, he said, "No."

Sam looked at Darryl for a moment. Darryl sat slumped over with his face buried in his hands.

Sam tried to comfort his best friend, "Hey now, buddy, I'm sure everything is gonna be all right. Don't let it bother you like this." He patted Darryl on his back.

Just then, Macy stepped into the room. With a smile she said, "All right guys, everything came back clear. You're both free to go."

Darryl looked up at Macy and back to Sam, ready to get to his house and explain everything to Ann. He only feared it was too late to reconcile. Darryl stood up after Sam. They followed Macy down the long hall to the lobby of the police station.

Once there, Macy explained, "I can give you guys a ride home, if you'd like. It'd be a long walk, otherwise."

Sam asked, "Would it be all right to take me back to my truck at the dock? I'd like to call somebody and get what's left of my boat."

Macy nodded and said, "Yeah, that's no problem." She looked at Darryl and asked, "Do you want to be dropped off with him?"

Darryl replied, "Would it be much trouble for you to take me to my house after you drop Sam off? I really need to get home to my wife."

Macy continued to smile as she said, "Yeah! That's no problem at all. I'd say she's worried sick about you." She motioned with her head as she said, "Let's get going." She walked toward the door with Sam close behind. Darryl stood for a moment as Macy's words settled on him.

"Not so much worried; I'd say she's just sick of me," he whispered to himself.

The morning sun made its way over the mountaintop as Macy drove Sam back to the dock. After she dropped him off to take care of his boat and take his truck home, she and Darryl continued on to Darryl's house. As they approached his driveway, everything seemed to be normal. The car still sat there in its usual spot.

As the patrol car came to a stop, Darryl made no movement to exit.

"You said it was this house, right?" asked Macy.

Still looking at his house, he dreaded the walk inside. "Yeah," Darryl sighed as he grasped the door handle. "Thanks for the ride."

Macy watched Darryl as he opened the door.

"Hey, it was no problem." She smiled. "You guys be more careful next time and stay out of trouble."

Sam stared blankly toward the house as he replied, "We will." He closed the door and walked up the driveway. Macy pulled away as Darryl approached the front door. He stood there for a moment as he prepared himself for the argument of his life. With everyone still asleep, the neighborhood seemed very quiet.

Darryl reached into his pocket and pulled out the keys. They jangled as his hand quivered while trying to unlock the door. After the door unlocked, Darryl tightly held the handle as he took in one last deep breath. He twisted the knob and pushed; the door swung open. Darryl peeked inside and looked around. He carefully took one step into the house, and then another. Silence filled the rooms as he closed the door behind him.

"Ann?"

Darryl gazed down the hall into the kitchen. He called her name again as he stopped at the bottom of the stairs.

The stillness persisted.

Darryl walked into the kitchen where he saw a single piece of paper laying on the counter. He walked to it and recognized Ann's handwriting covered the entire sheet. Darryl picked it up and read her heartbreaking words as he walked back into the living room. He sat on the couch as he read of Ann's hurt and resentment toward him. She said she would never come back and to expect divorce papers in the mail. After reading the final words of Ann's letter, Darryl's head fell back as he cupped his hands over his face. Darryl cried uncontrollably. He found it hard to believe it came to this. After everything he sacrificed and did for her, she just left.

He sat there for nearly an hour when a slow, pounding knock rattled the front door and startled Darryl. He tried to wipe the tears that covered his face while he gathered himself together and opened the door. Surprised, he saw three men standing there with slicked back hair, sickly-pale complexions, and dressed in black business suits with dark sunglasses.

Before Darryl could utter a word, the man that stood nearest to the door said in a monotone voice, "Darryl Matthew Stevenson, we need to speak to you about the events which occurred last night between the time frame of 10:29 P.M. and 11:27 P.M."

Aggravated, Darryl replied, "Listen, I filled out a report for you guys already. I don't want to talk about it anymore."

The man insisted, "Sir, we need you to come with us."

Darryl rolled his eyes and grew very angry. "Look, I told you! I filled out your report. I got home this morning and found out that my wife has left me. I'm really not in the mood to talk about anything right now!"

Unconcerned by Darryl's situation, the man said, "Sir, we are not affiliated with your local law enforcement in any way."

Darryl seemed to be very confused by the man's words. "Then, who are you with?"

The man stated, "Mr. Stevenson, we will be asking the questions. Now, please come with us *willingly*."

Darryl felt challenged and said, "Willingly? I just told you, I'm not going anywhere. You can get off of my property right now!"

The man turned his head back toward the two men that stood behind him. "Begin decontamination." All at once, the other two men approached Darryl and grabbed his arms. Darryl struggled, but the men were much stronger. They forced handcuffs around Darryl's wrists, lifted him by his arms, and carried him outside. Just as they exited the house, three other men that looked exactly like the others stormed inside. They carried red plastic gas jugs. They poured gasoline all throughout the house as the others carried Darryl toward a black van that sat behind a black sedan beside the road in front of Darryl's house. Another pale man in the same black suit stood near the back of the van.

Darryl continued to struggle as he glanced back at his house. He saw the three men no longer carried the red gas jugs as they walked out of the house. While the three walked toward the black sedan, Darryl saw the original man he talked to pull a white handkerchief and a Zippo lighter from the inside of his coat pocket.

"Hey! Stop! What do you think you're doing?" yelled Darryl as he tried to fight the grip the others had on him.

The man standing at the front door held the handkerchief out and lit it. Once the flame started to rise on the white cloth, he tossed it inside Darryl's home. Darryl watched in horror as his life erupted in flames.

The man that stood next to the van opened the back door; the others packed Darryl inside. Darryl was shocked to see Sam sitting in the back of the van, locked to a seat.

"Sam! What's going on?" asked Darryl as the men overpowered him and locked his legs and arms to a seat.

Sam's voice cracked as he replied, "I don't know

what these idiots think they're doing!"

Sam was scared and seemed to be on the verge of breaking down. Once the men in black suits locked Darryl into place, they exited the van. Darryl and Sam looked at Darryl's house–fire engulfed the entire two-story home. The men slammed the back doors of the van shut. Darryl and Sam sat speechless and looked at each other. They feared what the men planned to do next as they heard the doors of the sedan and the van shut. Both vehicles started up and began to drive away.

Later that night on the local news, the anchorman reported a very tragic accident had occurred early that morning.

"A tragic house fire claimed the lives of two Pikeville men earlier this morning. Fire Chief Ron Adkins told reporters Darryl Stevenson and Sam Howard were asleep in Stevenson's home when the fire began. Eyewitnesses told reporters Stevenson and Howard got back during the middle of the night from a fishing trip. Stevenson's wife wasn't home at the time of the fire and has declined to talk to reporters. Investigators concluded the fire was caused by an electrical malfunction in the home's wiring. The bodies of Stevenson and Howard were never recovered. Memorial services will be held for the two men tomorrow at the Pikeville Funeral Home."

THE HEIST

Here, let me have a go at it for a while, Josiah." said Ronnie as he reached for the shovel in Josiah's blistered hands.

Josiah let out a long breath as he shoveled the last scoop of dirt and sandstone onto the pile they'd deposited on the surface.

"Whew," gasped Josiah, running his filthy fingers through his dark brown hair. He handed the shovel up to Ronnie and climbed out of the chest-deep hole. He let his fatigued body fall to the ground a few feet away, right next to the spot his Winchester rifle and water canteen laid. "How much further do we got to go?"

Ronnie jumped into the hole and started digging at the dirt like a mad man. "It shouldn't be much further now." His huge arm muscles bulged as he tore chunk after chunk of the earth from itself.

Josiah knew Ronnie was telling the truth once he saw the enormous vein start to protrude out the side of his bald head. Ronnie would never work himself that hard unless there was going to be a big payoff for it. There would indeed be a handsome reward once they had Minnie Cratchet's body dug up. She was the wife of the richest man in Whittlersfield, Sammy Cratchet. Word got around town that Sammy had her buried with a ridiculous amount of expensive jewelry. Josiah and Ronnie were very eager to pay a visit to her grave.

Josiah uncorked the beat-up metal canteen and placed it to his dry lips. A rush of relief swam down his throat as he chugged the water as fast as he could. He then raised it high above himself and poured the soothing liquid all over his sweaty head. As Josiah looked up, he noticed how dark the sky appeared. The moon and stars were nowhere to be seen across the vast nothingness above them.

"It sure is cloudy out tonight, ain't it?"

Ronnie, still hard at work digging scoop-by-scoop closer to their prize grunted, "Yep."

"Ya know, my grandpaw told me a story one time about nights like this." Josiah looked over at Ronnie in the grave. Dirt flew out of it at an impressive rate. "Used to creep me out when I was little."

He paused. "Still does."

"That so?"

"Yeah. He said, when the nights are at their darkest like tonight, things of the devil come out to play. He swore he saw some of the craziest stuff around here at nighttime." Josiah picked the lantern up off the ground, held it high in the air, and looked around him.

"Josiah! Quit messin' around and keep that light shinin' over here! I can't see a thing I'm diggin' at!"

Josiah snapped back around and placed the lantern back where it was. "Here!"

"All right, keep it sittin' there! We ain't got time to mess around. There's probably just a few hours left 'til mornin,' and we gotta get this done tonight." Ronnie struck at the ground again and continued digging even harder.

Josiah stood still for a moment as he watched Ronnie. He didn't want to do anything else to upset him. Josiah felt a single drop of water land on top of his head. "Uh-oh"

Ronnie stopped digging as he looked up at the sky. "That's great. Just what we needed–rain!" He shook his head and drove the shovel into the ground.

The raindrops increased in intensity until it became a steady drizzle. The light of the lantern flickered once and disappeared. Ronnie cursed aloud.

"What do ya want me to do, Ronnie?"

Ronnie glanced over his shoulder and hollered, "Get in here and help me dig!"

Josiah jumped into the grave with his back to Ronnie. He bent over and scratched at the dirt with his hands. The duo dug frantically, trying to reach Minnie's coffin in the dark. The rain soon turned the dirt into mud.

"I don't know if this is worth all of the trouble, Ronnie!"

A hollow thump came from the ground as Ronnie wedged the shovel into the soft ground. A grin crept across Josiah's face as he turned toward Ronnie.

"You're about to see, my friend, exactly how much this was worth it." Ronnie laughed hysterically. He scraped the thin layer of mud and rocks away from the wooden coffin's top. "Dig around the sides!"

Josiah ran his hands around the coffin so a small ditch bordered the edges. Ronnie pushed the sharp edge of his shovel between the lid and the wall of the coffin. Josiah held himself over it by placing both feet on opposite sides of the grave as Ronnie pried the lid off.

The putrid stench of rotting flesh immediately filled the air as Ronnie started to separate the lid from the wooden tomb. Josiah gagged as he held his nose.

"Oh Lord! I can't believe I let you talk me into this"

"Trust me, buddy, it's all gonna be worth it."

With one more hard push on the shovel, the lid quickly popped up and fell back down.

"Help me lift this outta here," said Ronnie as he threw the shovel up to the ground above them. Both men grabbed one side of the lid and raised it above their heads. With a mighty shove, the lid landed topside up on the grass.

Ronnie lit a match and held his hand over it to shield it from the rain. Josiah looked down in disgust as Ronnie moved the match toward Minnie's rotten corpse. Most of the flesh on her face was rotted away, revealing the facial bones of her skull. A little hair remained atop her head in sparse patches. Maggots scattered from her neck and from underneath her flower-patterned dress when Ronnie moved the light down to reveal three gold necklaces resting on her chest.

"Oh yeah, there we go," said Ronnie as he moved his hand away from the flame. The light diminished, leaving them in darkness once again.

Ronnie struck another match and quickly moved it to her partially decayed hands. Minnie's fingernails were brown and chipped. Her left hand laid over her right. Josiah quickly noticed the gold wedding band on her ring finger and other assorted diamond rings on her other fingers.

The rain moved out just as Ronnie shook the match and threw it to the side.

Ronnie pointed up and said, “Go see if you can get that lantern lit again.”

Josiah put his slender forearms on the grass at the grave’s edge and pulled himself out. He turned and snatched the small box of matches Ronnie held in the air. After a few tries, Josiah had the lantern blazing. He grabbed it and held it over the grave for Ronnie to see. Minnie’s rotten corpse looked even more gruesome in the luminous light. The cruel shadows accented her hollow eye sockets and rotten neck.

Ronnie bent over and started fidgeting with Minnie’s decayed fingers. He slid four of the rings off with ease. Her left pinky rested on the edge of her right hand. It was bent, and Ronnie struggled to remove the last ring from the stiff, curved finger.

“Why, you stubborn little booger. Come off of there,” said Ronnie. He twisted and tugged on the ring with futile results. Josiah could tell Ronnie was getting very aggravated. Ronnie stopped and stood there for a second. “Well, there’s more than one way to skin a cat.” He forcefully grabbed her pinky and started to twist it.

Josiah cringed at the sound of Minnie’s bone snapping apart.

Ronnie turned around with a giant smile on his face, holding Minnie’s crumbling pinky between his thumb and index finger. “Looky here, Josiah! It looks like a wrinkled little caterpillar.”

Josiah gritted his teeth and closed his eyes. “That’s just sick.”

All of a sudden, just up the hill, the two horses they rode on to the gravesite began panicking. They were still tied to a couple of trees where they left them.

Josiah turned the lantern toward the horses and held it up to see what was the matter. "What in blazes is going on with them?" He squinted his eyes past the lantern and tried to focus on the distance in the darkness.

Ronnie craned his head out of the grave and held his hand up, trying to block the glare of the lantern from his eyes. "I bet it's a pack of coyotes over there after them." He quickly reached down and tore the gold necklaces from Minnie's body. After stuffing them into his pocket, Ronnie jumped up and pulled himself out of the grave.

Josiah and Ronnie snatched their guns up from the ground and ran toward the horses. Ronnie held his pistol in the air and fired two shots, hoping to spook the coyotes away.

"Get outta here, you mangy devils!" he shouted.

By the time the men reached them, the horses were still screaming and bucking. Josiah ran around the horses with the lantern still held high and his rifle pointed in front of him.

"Go on! Get!" he screamed. He popped off a shot into the darkness, hoping to shoot one of them or at least scare them off. Josiah hung the lantern on a broken branch of the tree his horse was tied.

Ronnie was inspecting his horse's legs as he said, "Looks like they got Lady's leg pretty good."

Josiah slung his rifle onto his shoulder and walked over to have a look at the horse's injuries.

"They sure did, didn't they?" Josiah gently touched Lady just above a deep gash in her front leg. He looked up into Lady's eyes and patted her neck. "She's gonna be all right. She's a tough girl."

Ronnie let out a heavy sigh. "We best be movin'

on outta here." He untied Lady from the tree.

Josiah raised his eyebrows. "Ronnie, ain't we even gonna cover Minnie back up first?"

"Ain't got time, Josiah. We better go before it gets light out."

Josiah's mouth hung open. "We can't just leave her body like that! What if those coyotes come back?"

Ronnie shrugged his shoulders as he buckled his holster around his waist. "Oh well. That ain't our problem now, is it?"

Out of nowhere, a piercing screech came from the darkness close by in the forest. Josiah's blood ran cold as he ripped his rifle from his shoulder. Ronnie held his pistol out as he frantically looked around them.

"What was that?" Ronnie whispered.

Josiah's heart felt like it was about to beat out of his chest. "Ronnie, I know you probably ain't in the mood to hear another of my grandpaw's stories, but he told me a story about that very sound."

"Shut up, Josiah! I don't wanna hear another one of your grandpaw's drunken tales. There's somethin' in them woods right now." Ronnie pointed his gun and fired another shot. "Get outta here!"

The squall unexpectedly echoed through the forest once again.

"I'm telling you, he knew what he was talking about! Didn't you just hear that thing? It was real, wasn't it?"

Out of the corner of his eye, Josiah saw a white figure scurrying on its hands and feet toward them. He turned to face the pale-skinned beast. Its wide eyes faintly glowed in the lantern's light, and in the middle of the humanoid face were two slender nostril holes. The hairless creature wailed as it rushed toward them, revealing the long, pointed teeth inside its mouth. Josiah noticed the creature's lean body and wondered how it could move at such a blazing speed. He raised his rifle at the monster and fired a shot. The creature abruptly darted to its left, back into the cover of darkness.

"Dear Lord, what was that thing?" yelled Ronnie. Beads of sweat glistened all over his face and head. His eyes were locked in a panicked stare toward the creature's last whereabouts.

Josiah tried to calm his own nerves as he reloaded his Winchester.

"My grandpaw was right, Ronnie!" He snapped the gun ready and held it against his cheek. "He called that thing a Deadin!"

"How do you even know that's what he was talking about?"

Just then, the Deadin let out another high-pitched wail from somewhere in the darkness that surrounded them. Josiah and Ronnie flinched.

"That's one reason right there. And, didn't you see the way it looked? It's exactly like he told me."

Josiah followed the sound of rustling leaves and snapping twigs with the end of the gun barrel until the sound came to a sudden stop. Ronnie froze while pointing his gun at the shadows.

"You see it anywhere?" His eyes glanced back and forth.

Josiah held still, listening for the Deadin.

"I'm not sure, I think it's over there," he whispered.

Branches started to move in the tree behind them, and before either of the men had time to react, the Deadin grabbed Ronnie's leg. Ronnie screamed as the

Deadin growled and sunk its dagger-like teeth into his thigh. He immediately pointed and shot his .45 at the monster. It squealed in agony as a burst of solid black blood sprayed from its bony back. The Deadin let go, but only for a moment. It pounced forward and resumed the attack on Ronnie's leg.

Josiah was afraid to shoot the Deadin; he worried the buckshot would hit Ronnie. He rushed at the Deadin and kicked it right under the ribs, knocking it back. The monster swung its long claws at Josiah. The beast barely missed slicing Josiah's stomach as he jumped backwards. Spotting his chance, Josiah fired a wad of buckshot at the Deadin's head. The back of its skull exploded in a mist of dark blood and brain matter. The ferocious monster's body fell limp and collided with the ground.

Josiah looked the monster over while still aiming his rifle. It appeared to be around five feet tall. The Deadin's hands had three fingers and a thumb, each with sharp, pointed claws. The skin that covered its body was so pale, dark veins were clearly visible. Josiah saw the blood smeared all around its mouth, and then he glanced over at Ronnie.

"You all right?"

He lowered the gun and ran to his friend's side. The Deadin had torn a large chunk of muscle from the back of Ronnie's leg. Josiah felt dizzy once he saw Ronnie's femur deep inside the wound.

"Oh no." Josiah looked at Ronnie's pale face. "I've gotta get you to Doctor Samson."

Ronnie was losing a lot of blood. He reached into his pocket and held out the necklaces and rings.

"Here. You hold on to these."

Josiah took the ball of jewelry and walked to his horse, Hector, to put the loot into the small cloth bag he had tied to the saddle. As Josiah pulled the bag open, he heard the unexpected screech of a Deadin, followed by Ronnie screaming for dear life. Josiah immediately turned and saw a Deadin on Ronnie's back. Ronnie tried to reach the nimble monster over his shoulders, but couldn't. The beast had its clawed toes dug deep into his sides. Ronnie cried out as he stumbled around, wrestling to get it off. With its mouth wide open, the Deadin reared its head back and sank its teeth into Ronnie's neck. It growled and hissed as it tore the flesh from his body.

Immediately, another Deadin bounded out of the darkness like some mutated cat. It helped the other Deadin bring Ronnie to the ground and tore into him at once. Josiah couldn't believe his eyes as he continued to watch more and more Deadin swiftly emerge from the shadows. They soon began attacking Ronnie's horse, too. The awful sounds of screeching Deadin, along with Ronnie and Lady's cries as they were being eaten alive filled the night air.

Josiah knew there was nothing he could do to save his partner. The only thing left to do was get out with his own life while he could. He grabbed the lantern, untied Hector from the tree, and mounted him.

"He-yah," he yelled as he kicked the horse.

By then, ten Deadin had huddled around Ronnie and Lady's bodies. Josiah whipped the reigns and urged Hector to go faster as they raced down the muddy trail. Hector galloped at a furious speed. Josiah held the swinging lantern up as Hector maneuvered through the winding turns. Josiah had a hard time seeing where they were going, but he placed all trust into his mighty steed.

A chill ran down Josiah's spine when he heard the wicked shriek of a Deadin close behind him. He turned to see a lone Deadin running on its hands and feet chasing Hector through the trail. Out of sheer terror, Josiah tossed the lantern at his pursuer. It smashed in a small ball of fire on the ground in front of the Deadin, but the creature jumped to the side and avoided the fireball. It was gaining ground on them. Josiah reached over his shoulder to grab his Winchester. The moment Josiah readied his gun against his shoulder and aimed, he was knocked from his horse by a low-hanging branch. He hit the ground with a great impact.

As Josiah lay there in the mud, stunned and in pain, he listened to the sounds of Hector's thundering hooves and the wails of the Deadin fade into the distance. The moon shone through the clouds, providing a small amount of light. It was just enough for Josiah to see his surroundings. Once Josiah could no longer hear Hector, he struggled to crawl to a secure area with his rifle. Off the trail, he leaned his back against the trunk of a large tree. Josiah struggled to catch his breath after having the wind knocked out of him.

Just as Josiah felt a brief sense of safety, he heard the sloppy sounds of bare feet beating against the muddy trail coming toward him. The wet slaps were in a rhythm of four beats. He tightly clenched the rifle in his hands, knowing his one remaining shell could take care of just one of the horrid creatures. Josiah sat still as he listened to the creature get closer. He held his breath as the footsteps galloped past him.

Josiah slowly exhaled a sigh of relief. He was so overwhelmed with emotions, tears started to swell up in his eyes. He closed his eyes as he sobbed uncontrollably. He grieved for his friend and silently asked for forgiveness for the horrible things he had done that night.

In an instant, Josiah felt his heart stop as a few gentle puffs of air blew against his face, accompanied by a sniffing sound. He opened his eyes to discover a Deadin looking him in the eyes. Josiah panicked and did the first thing that came to his mind. He shot his final bullet without aiming it, whatsoever. The buckshot burst into the sky from the barrel. The Deadin pinned Josiah against the tree and tore into his throat with its razor-sharp teeth. Blood gushed from Josiah's mouth as three other Deadin joined in. Each of them tore his body apart in a feeding frenzy. He could hear more Deadin screeching as they made their way to him. Josiah watched the twenty or so Deadin surround him, fighting for any morsel of his own body. At last, the searing pain of claws had penetrated his skull and put an end to the grave robber's final heist–the Deadin ripped Josiah's head from his shoulders.

ABOUT THE AUTHOR

Jason Thacker was born in Pikeville, Ky and still resides in the mountains of Eastern Kentucky with his wife, Tiffany, and their three dogs, Rusty the Cairn, Bella the Scottie, and Rocko the Doberman/Lab mix. He credits his interest in writing to a lifelong love for comics, books, and movies.

In June 2012 Jason released his first novel, **Dead Are Alive: A Zombie Western Novel.**

FIND JASON ONLINE

Website:
jasonthacker.wordpress.com

Facebook:
www.facebook.com/authorjasonthacker

Twitter:
@jason_thacker

Also from Jason Thacker:
Dead Are Alive

Following a church robbery and the murder of reverend Hopkins' wife, Gwen, bounty hunter Fred Douglas tries to bring justice to the corrupt town of Hazel by assassinating Gwen's murderer, Sheriff Wellman.

As Fred awaits his execution after a failed attempt on the sheriff, an experimental antivenom reanimates two children into the unmercifully ravenous walking dead. Chaos erupts as the children begin a bloody feeding frenzy. The virus is spread with every bite and before long their victims rise from the bloody earth to join a swelling horde.

In this western town, there's no longer a choice of bringing down criminals dead or alive. Because this time, the dead are alive!

"Imagine riding shotgun with the Wild Bunch on a nightmare ride through zombie country and you've got a pretty good idea of the terror Jason Thacker has cooked up in Dead Are Alive. Thacker's latest left me breathless and begging for more. Trust me, not since Joe R. Lansdale's Dead in the West has the Old West been this scary!"

-Joe McKinney, **Bram Stoker Award-winning author of Flesh Eaters** and **Dead City**.

www.ingramcontent.com/pod-product-compliance
Lightning Source LLC
Chambersburg PA
CBHW070505130626
46555CB00003B/1174

9780692276686